SHORT LIST

Also by Jim Lehrer

• • •

Books

LOST AND FOUND

THE SOONER SPY

CROWN OKLAHOMA

KICK THE CAN

WE WERE DREAMERS

VIVA MAX

Plays

CHILI QUEEN

CHURCH KEY CHARLIE BLUE

SHORT LIST

. . .

JIM LEHRER

G. P. PUTNAM'S SONS
New York

G. P. Putnam's Sons
Publishers Since 1838
200 Madison Avenue
New York, NY 10016

The author acknowledges permission to reprint lyrics from "God Bless
America," copyright © 1938 by Irving Berlin, copyright renewed.
Copyright assigned to Joe DiMaggio, Anne Phipps Sidamon-Eristoff,
and Theodore R. Jackson as Trustees of the God Bless America Fund.
International copyright secured. Used by permission. All rights reserved.

Library of Congress Cataloging-in-Publication Data

Lehrer, James.
Short list / Jim Lehrer.
p.   cm.
ISBN 0-399-13665-7
I. Title.
PS3562.E4419S48   1992   91-472 CIP
813'.54—dc20

Printed in the United States of America
1   2   3   4   5   6   7   8   9   10

This book is printed on acid-free paper.
∞

To Aunt Grace, Uncle Paul and GaGa

• • •

1

. . .

OKLAHOMA PARTS

I'd like to tell you about the time I was on the Short List—
the Short List to be the Democratic nominee for vice-president of the United States. It was an unusual event because I
was both the first one-eyed American and the first Oklahoman
of any kind ever to come really close to being nominated for
national office. The whole experience lasted barely two days
and it caused some extreme difficulties for me, my family
and a lot of other people. But it *did* happen and, on balance,
I am glad it did.

I was the lieutenant governor of Oklahoma at the time. It
was a job I loved and cherished, and even Republicans and
The Daily Oklahoman agreed I performed very well. I had
never even given too many thoughts to running for governor
of Oklahoma, much less for vice-president of the whole country, because Buffalo Joe Hayman, our governor, was the
Sooner man of destiny at the time. He was supposed to make
it to the Short List to be a possible candidate for vice-president,

9

for Second Man of America. Not me. A burst blood vessel in a brain, plus a nod and a few words from David Brinkley, changed that all around.

It began with Joe's sending word through our secretaries that he had some important word on the sun. *The* sun.

My very small office was right around the corner from his very large office on the second floor of the state capitol building. I was there in a flash.

He was standing with his back to the door, looking past the pumping Chevron oil well on the capitol grounds to the skyline of downtown Oklahoma City and points south.

Joe was a tall, bulky man with linen-white skin and dark brown hair who wore white shirts, dark brown suits and black ties. He was from Buffalo, Oklahoma, out in the Panhandle, and his nickname "Buffalo Joe" came from that, although there were some who said it was also because he resembled a buffalo. Not me. I did not say that.

Now he turned from the window to me. His head was slanted upward slightly. His eyes were closed.

"It's happened, Mack. It's happened. Do you see the tan? Do you see it?"

I said I saw it.

He opened his eyes and pointed toward the phone on his desk. "Mark T. Andrews just called me. The speaker of the U.S. House of Representatives Mark T. Andrews. The chairman of the Democratic National Convention Mark T. Andrews. He asked me to keynote the convention, Mack. He asked me to give the keynote speech at the Democratic National Convention in New York City three weeks from this coming Monday. It happened, Mack. Oklahoma's day in the sun has finally arrived, in this Year of Our Lord 1976, this Bicentennial Year of Our Nation, the Greatest Nation on

Earth. It has finally arrived, Mack. Look again at this face. Look again."

I looked again at his white face.

"What do you see, Mack? What do you see?"

"I see tan, Joe."

I went over and shook his hand.

"What size shirt do you wear, Mack?" he asked.

"Sixteen–thirty-three," I replied.

"I think we have one for you. It's there on the desk."

I walked to the desk and picked up a light brown dress shirt still folded and pinned and wrapped in cellophane. It was an Arrow shirt from Buffalo Dry Goods, Buffalo, Oklahoma.

Joe explained:

"My mother asked me what I wanted for my birthday, which as you and all Oklahoma know is still five months away. I told her a brown shirt to wear on weekends to barbecues. She asked me my size. I said seventeen and a half–thirty-six. That's exactly what I said. Seventeen and a half–thirty-six. So yesterday that shirt arrives. I called her. Mom, I said. Mom, I said seventeen and a half–thirty-six was my size, and you sent me a sixteen–thirty-three. She said, They didn't have any brown ones in your size, son. No brown ones in your size, son. That's what she said. She bought that shirt because it was brown, even though it was the wrong size and I can't wear it."

"It's the thought that counts, Joe."

"No, it isn't, Mack. No, it isn't. On shirts it's the size. It really is the size. It is not the thought. Not on shirts."

I nodded or did something in agreement and started to take my leave. But there was something else. With Buffalo Joe, there was often Something Else.

He said:

"Mack, this incredible Keynote Address development means I need a favor from you right this very minute. I need to begin immediately considering courses of action. What kind of suit and tie and shirt should I wear when I mount that podium at that Madison Square Garden? Everybody in politics is wearing dark blue suits with wine ties and white shirts these days. Have you noticed that, Mack? Have you noticed that? I have. The successful ones notice things like that. The question is, do I want to be like everybody? I hate dark blue suits, Mack. I do not wear them. I wear brown, Mack. I wear brown because I like brown. Am I everybody or am I somebody else? What do I wear, then? Well, I have got to start immediately on this kind of thing. Immediately. And the speech. It's got to be the speech of my life, the speech of Oklahoma's life. I have got to start thinking right now about who is going to write it. Right now."

He stopped for a second. I had no idea what was coming, but I knew I was not going to like it.

"Iwo, Mack. You have got to do the Iwo ribbon-cutting thing this afternoon."

"No, Joe! Please!"

"You are the Second Man of Oklahoma, Mack. Your job is to be there when the First Man needs you. The First Man needs you to do Iwo."

"You know how much I hate war, Joe."

"I hate war, too, Mack. Roosevelt hated war. Everybody hates war. But this is only playing war."

"It's not another C.R.A.P. deal, is it?"

He smiled slightly and said, "No, sir. We have checked it out. It's all up-and-up and straight. And you can use The Limo. The Limo, Mack. Did you hear me? You can use The Limo."

I heard him.

"How you coming on the Movie Thing?" was his final question.

"Slowly," was my final answer.

The Limo wasn't really a limo, the movie wasn't a real movie, and Iwo wasn't the real Iwo.

The Limo was a standard dark blue Chrysler Imperial four-door sedan the State of Oklahoma provided for the governor, along with two highway patrolmen in plain clothes— one to drive, the other to keep a lookout for potential kidnappers and terrorists. I didn't get to use it much except when Joe was out of the state and I was acting governor, but I loved it when I did. It made me feel like I mattered, which was not always the case as I went about my regular every-day, every-minute duties as lieutenant governor of Oklahoma.

The Movie Thing was *Oklahoma Parts*, starring Melody Anderson as Mary Belle Beloit, a University of Oklahoma physics instructor, and Scott Crowe as Bob T. Walker, the president of Oklahoma Northern State College. Our tax-funded Oklahoma Movie Production Assistance Administration, called "Oompah" around the capitol, had turned Sooner heaven and earth to help the moviemakers find locations, facilities, extras and everything else they needed. The Oompah people said they had seen a rough treatment of the movie beforehand which had laid out an old-fashioned boy-meets-girl film of mostly wholesomeness and goodness that would be great for the image of Oklahoma. But when the shooting had begun in Enid, it had turned out to be a short X-rated film with front and rear nudity, explicit oral and regular sex, plus many other awful and dirty things. Joe, worried as always about bad publicity and the Baptist fallout, had given me the assignment of solving the problem. "Clean it up or kill it, Mack," he had said. Yes, sir, I had replied.

But first—right now—there was Iwo. Iwo as in Iwo Jima, the Pacific Island that had been the scene of a bloody battle and the famous flag-raising on a mountain called Suribachi in World War II. One of the U.S. Marines who had gone ashore in Iwo and returned to tell about it was Gunnery Sergeant Bertram Leroy Upchurch of Sylvester, Oklahoma. Everybody called him Gunny. He had come back to Sylvester to prosper as a John Deere tractor and farm implement dealer. Now in his mid-sixties, Gunny had sold his business to create a most unusual public attraction on 112 acres of flat farm-land sixty-five miles south of Oklahoma City at Exit 22 on Interstate 35. He called it Iwo and claimed it was Oklahoma's first participatory war-game facility.

The C.R.A.P. worry, by the way, was about an awful thing that had happened to me in the town of Rocker, Oklahoma, a few months before. Rocker was a tiny place in the Pan-handle, and like now, as a last-minute replacement for Joe, I had gone there to cut a ribbon. It was to open a plant for converting cattle manure to natural gas, and eventually to other useful things like potting soil and cat litter. The plant would employ 150 to 175 Oklahomans, so it was considered a vital addition to Panhandle Process, Inc., which sounded important and scientific enough. It wasn't until I got there and actually saw the name on the side of the new factory that would employ 150 to 175 Oklahomans that I realized the company initials were C.R.A.P.

After the ribbon-cutting I had joined the whole town at an Opening Day Festival in the Rocker High School gym. There had been light refreshments and country singing and dancing, and finally, in honor of the plant and to demonstrate one more use for cow manure, a game of what they call Cow

Chip Bingo. Cow Chip Bingo. They had sectioned off half the gym floor into numbered yard squares. Each of us had chosen one of the numbered squares, like it was a big bingo card. Then a kid in a blue Future Farmers of America jacket had brought a live cow in on a leash and walked it around on the squares. Where the cow delivered a chip—where she C.R.A.P.ed—was the winning square. This particular cow had been reliable and fast. It had taken her only a minute or two to drop a chip the first time. We played five more times before I was able to convince my hosts that I had important state business to tend to back in Oklahoma City.

It had been the most unusually miserable time I had ever had in the service of my state. I thought of it again in all its detail as I sat in the backseat of The Limo speeding down the Exit 22 ramp on the way to cut the ribbon at Iwo.

We had no trouble finding it. There were huge signs along I-35 and on the county blacktop road to the entrance. "Be a Hero at Iwo!" they said in foot-high red letters. Then, in smaller yellow ones, "Participate in Realistic Reenactment of World War II Battle" and, under that in olive green, "All Equipment Furnished. $15 per Person. Special Group Rates." There was a larger-than-life painted wood portrait of a Marine in full battle dress on the left side of the front gate, and one of the famous Mount Suribachi flag-raisers on the right.

Gunny Upchurch met us just inside. He was a short, square man with a small pillow belly and a megaphone voice who called everybody Skipper. He was dressed in camouflage dungarees, matching steel helmet and shiny brown combat boots, with a .45-caliber pistol in a brown leather holster on his right hip. His smiling face was blackened with some kind of smudge.

"Call me Gunny, Skipper," he said immediately.

"Call me Mack, Gunny," I replied immediately.

He pointed toward the black eyepatch I wear over my empty left eye socket. I had grown tired of people asking me about that.

"Lose it in combat, Skipper Mack?" he asked.

"Not really," I replied.

Gunny winked and smiled, and said, "Modesty is becoming in politicians because there ain't much of it, Skipper Mack."

And before I could correct any assumptions he might have made, he moved me right up to a microphone in the middle of a group of twenty-five or thirty people. Most of them were dressed and smudge-faced like him as Marines, but a few were small and wore uniforms of Japanese soldiers.

Gunny handed me a large bolo knife and pointed me toward a two-inch-wide red-and-yellow ribbon that hung across the door of a large silver World War II–type Quonset hut. "Have at it, sir," he said.

The bolo knife had a three-foot-long blade and a padded handle another foot in length. I had never seen, much less held, anything as big and deadly. It took both hands to raise it above my head and crash it downward. That poor ribbon never stood a chance. The blade zipped through it like it was warm ice cream.

There was a lot of clapping. I set the knife down and Gunny shook my right hand. Then he turned to his uni-formed Marines and Japanese soldiers and barked, "Move out!"

All of them were through the Quonset hut door and out of sight in a few seconds.

"Well," I said, reaching again for Gunny's right hand, "this has been a real pleasure. Congratulations. I have got to head back to the capital now."

Gunny wouldn't let go of my hand. "I can't let you go until you have run the course, Skipper Mack. The governor had already promised *he* would."

Sure. There was no way to decline.

He took me inside the Quonset hut to a small Uniform Room full of camouflage dungarees hanging from racks like at a Sears.

"Trouser size?" asked a young man of eighteen or so.

"Thirty-two waist, thirty-one inseam," I replied.

He handed me off the rack a pair of camouflage dungaree pants.

"Shirt?"

"Sixteen neck. Thirty-three sleeve."

He handed me a dungaree shirt.

"Shoe size?"

"Nine and a half C."

He gave me a pair of boots.

Then he ushered me into a tiny dressing room like you see in the men's clothing sections of department stores.

I stripped off my dark blue suit, blue button-down-collar Oxford-cloth shirt and the rest of my clothes, and slipped into the Marine outfit.

Gunny escorted me next door to the 7-82 Gear Room; "7-82 gear," I was told, was a Marine term. I was fitted for a steel helmet with camouflage cover and helmet liner, size seven and a half, and for a tan cartridge belt full of what Gunny said were clips of blank rifle ammunition. A canteen and a first-aid kit were hooked on the belt.

Finally, there was the Weapons Room. A man there handed me what he said was an M-1 rifle and showed me how to put in clips of blanks for firing.

By now we were at the back door of the Quonset hut.

Gunny and I stepped outside to the edge of a long ditch full of water about twenty feet wide.

"Think of this as the Pacific Ocean," said Gunny. "We're going to charge through it like out of landing craft to the beach. Do you read me, Skipper Mack?"

I read him, all right. He was a lunatic.

We were joined by a group of ten more lunatics dressed the same way we were. One of them came over to me and without a word spread black charcoal over my face. We made a twelve-abreast wave formation.

"That's Iwo over there, men," said Gunny in a voice that equaled John Wayne, Randolph Scott, John Payne and all the other great movie Marines of history.

Then he raised his right hand and screamed: "Charge!"

We took off running. The water was just under boot-top high. We splashed through it at top speed. Several of the others growled like wolves or hooted like wild savages.

Suddenly there was the sound of small-arms fire. A patch of dirt on the beach exploded in front of us.

"Yankee dogs die!" screamed a high-pitched voice in a mock Japanese accent.

"Hit it!" Gunny barked. He leaped spread-eagle onto the ground. So did the others. So did I. The ground was fresh sand—fresh from the back of a dump truck, obviously.

One of the little Japanese soldiers stood up from behind a mound of dirt. "Die, Melican Maline!" he yelled, as he opened fire with a machine gun. Gunny started firing his M-1. So did the others. So did I.

Two other Japanese soldiers showed themselves from behind a tree. They yelled and fired. We fired back.

They disappeared and Gunny ordered us to charge after them.

And so it went for the next forty-five minutes.

We'd advance through brush or trees or wheat fields or over fences until we met resistance from the Japanese. There would be a brief firefight and away we would go again. The Japanese always yelled at us. Occasionally, we'd hear the recorded female voice of a Tokyo Rose type urging us to surrender to the "vastly supelior forces of Impelial Army of Japan." Occasionally, some dirt would fly up in our faces with an explosion. Occasionally, we'd have to clean out a machine-gun nest or an artillery bunker.

Finally, we arrived at our objective, a manmade mini-mountain of high ground. Gunny picked up a flagpole with an American flag on it. The group and I took it and put it up, just like the real Marines had done at Mount Suribachi. One of Gunny's employees took our picture with a Polaroid camera. He presented the print to me.

"We could have used you there for the real thing, Skipper Mack," he said in a little ceremony, as the flag blew unfurled in the breeze and a recorded band rendition of the Marine Corps Hymn played.

Then we were joined by the Japanese soldiers, and there were introductions, handshakes, smiles and camaraderie all around.

"Look carefully at those Japs," Gunny said with pride.

I looked at them carefully. Their faces were made up to look Oriental. But there was a softness to them that was not quite right.

"They're girls from our high school, cheerleaders, things like that, who need some extra spending money," Gunny said when it was clear I had not figured it out for myself. "Girls are the only people in Oklahoma small enough to be Japs."

I congratulated him on his business wisdom and for what he had created here.

"There's nothing else like it, Skipper Mack," said Gunny.

"You may not believe it, but there's nowhere else in the world you can pay fifteen dollars, help retake Iwo Jima and go home with a Polaroid shot of you putting the flag atop Suribachi to prove it."

I believed him.

"I think I have created one more version of the gold mine, Mack. People are going to swarm in here like flies to honey, pigs to slop, politicians to cash—no offense."

I told him I agreed with him.

Normally, I would have told Jackie every little detail of something as strange and crazy as my afternoon at Iwo. Jackie was my wonderful, beautiful, brilliant, funny wife. There was nothing she enjoyed more than a good story from my labors as Second Man of Oklahoma. She had laughed and smiled and hooted off and on for three days after I had returned from Rocker and told her about C.R.A.P., for instance. Jackie was one of Oklahoma's leading businesswomen, and the two of us took particular pleasure in discussing new and/or unusual business ventures. But Iwo would be out-of-bounds for talk forever. Because of Pepper. Tom Bell Bowen, her first husband and my best friend, whose nickname had been "Pepper." He had been a Marine in the Korean War and had died a hero when he'd jumped on a hand grenade to save the lives of his comrades and been blown to bits.

Hey, Jackie, look at this photo of me in a Marine outfit with a bunch of lunatics putting up a flag in the middle of an oversized Oklahoma molehill! Hey, Jackie, let me tell you about how I splashed through a ditch and shot blanks at high school girls dressed up like Japanese soldiers! Hey, Jackie, how many customers would Gunny have to have each day to turn a profit, and what are his prospects for franchising war?

No way.

We had Buffalo Joe's big Keynote Address news to discuss. And before we got to that she had some news of her own. Big Business news.

Jackie was the founder and owner of JackieMarts Inc., America's first chain of drive-thru grocery stores. Her idea was to make it possible for people to buy groceries and other small convenience items without having to get out of their cars. She had devised a system based on how the fast-food people did it, where you gave your order at a microphone and then drove to a pick-up window. She had started with one store south of downtown Oklahoma City. There were now 586 of them in twelve states. It was a truly remarkable Oklahoma women-in-business success story.

Now she told me with great excitement about a telephone call she had received that afternoon from Hugh B. Glisan. He had been the manager of the Union Bus Station in Oklahoma City for several years, including the summer our son Tommy Walt had worked there as a baggage agent. Tommy Walt had not been cut out to be a bus baggage agent, and Glisan had been pretty understanding in helping us all through a difficult time. He had gone on to become the division superintendent for Continental Trailways in Memphis, and just a few months before, he had made assistant general manager and moved to the Continental Trailways general office in Dallas.

Jackie and I should have been alone together in our dining room. Her business had made it possible for us to live much better than my $9,000-a-year lieutenant governor's salary would have otherwise allowed. We had recently moved into a big two-story brick house in an area of Oklahoma City known as Heritage Hills, which was old, delightful and just north of downtown. Our dining room table could seat twelve people, when all of the leaves were in. But we seldom used it at any size. Usually we ate out, like we were doing this night at Michelangelo's, a linen-tablecloth Italian restaurant named after an artist. I had a Caesar salad without the anchovies, which I hated, and veal parmigiana, which was nothing more than a cutlet with cheese and tomato sauce on top, and a small side dish of spaghetti with butter sauce. Jackie had only a small house salad and something called gnocchi, which were little dumpling things made of potato.

"He said the president of Continental Trailways, a Mr. Hammerschmidt, had a billion-dollar idea," she said. "It would involve merging the resources of Trailways and National Parcel Delivery Service, NPDS, with JackieMarts to form a multipurpose service of the future."

"What does he mean by 'merging'?" I asked.

"That's what Hammerschmidt will talk about when he comes up here," Jackie said. "He wants to take you and me to dinner. Is the Park Plaza all right?"

"Fine with me," I said.

I was going to Enid in the morning, but I figured I would be able to clean up or kill *Oklahoma Parts*, drop by the Museum of the Cherokee Strip to see Sandra Faye Parsons about something else, and still make it back in time for dinner. I loved going to the Park Plaza.

Jackie had heard on the radio and then seen on TV about Buffalo Joe's being chosen to keynote the Democratic convention.

"They must be out of their minds," she said. "No wonder you Democrats always lose."

"Don't forget Kennedy and Johnson," I said.

She waved my line away with a movement of her fork. I followed it with the news that Joe was hoping his minutes in the national spotlight might lead to the vice-presidential nomination for him.

"Not even the Democrats are that stupid," she said. She took a bite of gnocchi, which were white pasty–looking, chewed carefully, swallowed and then added, "Are they, Mack?"

"Hush, please," I said with a tone of mock anger. "You are talking about the man who chose me and continues to choose me to be the Second Man of Oklahoma."

"Sorry," she said with a tone of mock apology. "I hope he gets somebody to write his speech who can read and write, so he doesn't embarrass all of Oklahoma all over national television and the Western world."

"Me, too," I said with a tone of straight hope.

2
· · ·
SOMEONE NATIONAL

Joe's Keynote Address selection was big news in Oklahoma. The newspapers and the television and radio stations had announced with pleasure and pride that our governor had been chosen to appear in the national spotlight. *The Daily Oklahoman* and *The Seminole Producer* went even further, suggesting that it could even lead to the first Sooner on a national ticket. "Give 'em your best shot in that speech, Joe," concluded the *Producer* editorial. "It could land you a wink and a smile away from the most powerful position on earth."

Joe had those and many other newspapers laid out on his desk at the capitol when I came in the next morning. I squinted my eyes and my mind and imagined him a wink and smile away from the most powerful position on earth. We've had worse, I said to myself.

"Cow agreed to write the speech," was what he said first, instead of hello or anything else. "Cow has agreed to write the speech!"

I knew who he meant. Cow Cowell was an immoral Oklahoma sportswriter-poet-novelist-gambler-drunk who lived with a girl half his age in Pauls Valley. His real first name was Marvin, but he was called Cow. I had heard of him but never met him. I had heard of him first when, several years before, he had written a stupid story about Oklahoma for an eastern magazine named *Harper's*. It was in verse, like a poem, and it made fun of us, our oil and our red dirt and our OU football team, and it particularly made fun of Buffalo Joe. There were lines like:

> *Oklahoma, where the wind comes sweeping down the plains,*
> *Where the governor's Joe, Joe, Buffalo Joe,*
> *Where the corn is as high as an elephant's eye,*
> *And a lot of it comes from Joe, Joe, Buffalo Joe.*

Joe hadn't minded. It was his first mention in a national magazine. "You take it the way you can get it, Mack," he had said. "Now the whole world knows Oklahoma has a governor named Joe."

Now I asked him why he had decided on a man who had made fun of him in a national magazine to write the most important speech of his life.

"Because Cow's national and I need someone national," said Joe.

"Isn't he also living in sin with a girl young enough to be his daughter?" I said sternly.

"Like I say, he's national."

I asked if he knew for a fact that Cow Cowell had ever written this kind of speech before.

"Not for a fact."

"You didn't ask him?"

"If you can write poetry and stories, you can write speeches," Joe said. "It's the same as singing."

The same as singing? Mario Lanza can sing "The Hugotown Hug" like Nita Pickens of Perkins Corner, Miss Country Music of the World? Nita Pickens of Perkins Corner can sing "O Sole Mio" like Mario Lanza?

"I wished you had," I said.

"Look, I gave Cow a week-from-today deadline for a first draft. I hereby appoint you to be in charge of riding herd on him to make sure he makes it. Thank you so much, Mack. Thank you so much."

"Hey, Joe, please!"

"Mack, when the First Man needs the Second Man, there is no greater need."

I remember very well that I did not expect to change anything, but I also remember that it seemed important to me to raise all of the flags and questions.

"What is it you said about garbage, Joe?" I said. "It's too late to burn it or bury it after you touch it." He had made that one up after a delegation from the city of Philadelphia, Pennsylvania, had come to see him about maybe buying up several hundred unused acres in western Oklahoma to use as a massive dump for its garbage and trash.

It didn't fit this situation exactly, and it didn't make a lot of sense, but he got the point.

"Aren't you off to Enid to kill a movie?" he said, meaning the meeting was over.

"Right. Iwo was an extraordinary experience, Joe. Not as bad as C.R.A.P. But a close second or third."

"Love to hear about it sometime, Mack. Love to."

He did not offer me the use of The Limo again. So I went off to Enid in my dark blue Buick Skylark to kill a movie and to see what Sandra Faye Parsons had on her mind. Sandra Faye was a historian who ran the Museum of the Cherokee Strip in Enid.

Enid, population 50,300, was a city of stories and mysteries. One of the best was just about its name. Many towns in Oklahoma were named by the railroads, and the story was that a man from the Rock Island had done Enid. He had been a big fan of Alfred, Lord Tennyson, the British poet I remembered from school for "The Charge of the Light Brigade." The Rock Island man had decided that Enid, the wife of a guy called Geraint in a book of Tennyson poems titled *Idylls of the King*, rated having an Oklahoma town named for her. So without consulting anybody but his bosses in Chicago, he had named Enid Enid. But that wasn't for sure. Another theory was that some cowboy on a drive along the Chisholm Trail had stopped at a spring there in this new settlement on the Cherokee Strip in the Oklahoma Territory and seen a sign on a cook's tent that said "Dine." The cowboy had turned the sign upside down so it said "Enid." And Enid it became and was from then on. The best thing was that nobody really knew which of these stories or any of a couple of others about how Enid had become Enid was true.

The saddest Enid story was definitely true and was right there as you drove in from Oklahoma City, Kingfisher, Hennessey, Waukomis and other points south on U.S. Highway 81. Off to the left behind the Best Western and other motels and small restaurants and service stations was Vance Air Force Base, a major training base for U.S. Air Force pilots. The sadness was in its name, Vance, for Lieutenant Colonel Leon R. Vance. He, like me, was born in Kansas, but his family had moved to Enid when he was four years old. He had graduated from Enid High School and then gone on to OU at Norman and finally to West Point. In the summer of 1944, he was twenty-eight years old and a B-24 Liberator group commander for the 8th Air Force in England. On a pre–D Day bombing mission over France, his command plane had been hit several times by antiaircraft fire. By the time it had circled back over the English Channel, three of its four engines had been knocked out, the pilot was dead, and Colonel Vance's right foot had been blown nearly loose from his leg. With his foot attached to his leg only by a thin piece of tendon, Vance crawled into the space next to the pilot's seat and tried to keep the plane flying. But then the fourth engine started to fail. He ordered the crew to bail out, which they did. But Vance thought—mistakenly, it turned out—there was at least one crew member on board who was too wounded to jump. So, still down there wedged in next to the pilot's seat, he belly-landed the plane on the water. There was an explosion that miraculously blew him free from the plane. Vance inflated his Mae West life jacket and grabbed onto a piece of the plane's wreckage. He hung on there for an hour before being rescued. He was saved. But the story did not end there. The awful, truly awful ending came several weeks later, on July 26, 1944, when he was put on a hospital evacuation plane for America. The plane disappeared somewhere between Iceland and Newfoundland. The remains of the plane and Colonel Vance were never found.

He, like Pepper, had been posthumously awarded a Congressional Medal of Honor. What my friend Tom Bell Pepper Bowen and Colonel Vance had done never, ever stopped amazing me. I always wondered what I would have done had I been Pepper or Colonel Vance. Or anyone else who did superhuman, heroic things just like that. Just like it was a natural thing to do. I was afraid it would not be natural with me. It was about the only time that I was glad I had only one eye. That meant I would never have to go to war and never have to find out for sure about myself.

On the morning I went to see Jed Berryhill at the Best Western, I was thinking about it all again. I could not help it. I saw the Vance Air Force Base sign and saw and heard jet fighter planes flying around overhead.

My appointment with Berryhill, producer of *Oklahoma Parts*, was for ten-thirty in the coffee shop of the Best Western where the film company was doing location shooting. I made the fortunate mistake of arriving a few minutes early and going not to the coffee shop but around the side, where there were big trucks and lights outside a motel room. I walked right up to the door of the motel room. It was open a couple of inches, so I peeked in. What I saw was two people, a middle-aged man of not less than fifty and a young woman of not more than twenty, sitting calmly on the edge of a bed, drinking coffee and eating what looked to be chocolate cake doughnuts. Neither had clothes on. Not one stitch.

"Mr. Berryhill?" I asked as I opened the door a foot or so.

The man looked over at me and said, "He just went to the restaurant." He made no effort to cover up any part of himself. Neither did the young woman, who was blonde and rather attractive. I assumed she was the actress Melody Anderson, playing the part of the OU physics instructor. He was black-haired, tanned and rather muscular. I assumed he was the actor named Scott Crowe, playing the part of the president of Oklahoma Northern State College. According to what the head of Oompah had told me, the awful story line involved the instructor's effort to get hired by ONSC as chairman of the physics department. It was a tenured position.

29

"Places!" somebody yelled. That somebody turned out to be a man in blue jeans and a blousy long-sleeved sport shirt. He walked over to me from a corner.

"We're making a movie here, sweetheart," he said to me. "If your need is Jed, then your need is elsewhere."

He turned back to the two people on the bed. "Okay, let's rehearse it one more time," he said. They groaned, and he said, "Then we bring the cameras in and do it for real. Okay. From the top."

I promise you what happened next was . . . well, more than I had ever witnessed in my life. The couple wrapped themselves in each other's legs, grabbed each other's breasts and swung back on the bed.

"Great moves, Scott," said the man in the blue jeans. "Smile, Melody. Smile. This is fun, remember. Fun!"

The couple twisted and turned, and finally they were having sexual intercourse in a way I was not familiar with. I will not describe it.

It took a few seconds for what was happening to sink in. When it did, I left in disgust for the coffee shop.

Jed Berryhill did not shake my hand. He wrestled with it with both of his.

"Guv, Guv," he said. "As Jimmy would say, I've never met a governor of Oklahoma I didn't like."

"I'm the lieutenant governor. Jimmy?"

"I haven't ever met one of those, either," he said, with a laugh that said it was another thing his life could probably have done without. "Let's make it Lewt Guv, then, okay? Jimmy Stewart. I worked on *The Glenn Miller Story* with him."

He laughed again and I smiled.

Berryhill was small, like an equipment manager for some

junior high B-team football squad. He was in his early fifties but clearly he wished he was another age. Maybe even *from* another age. His eyes were small and brown, his hair was uncombed and brown, his skin was pockmarked and tan. He was dressed in expensive-looking blue jeans and a light blue cashmere sweater with both sleeves pushed up on his arms above the elbow, like girls wear them. He wore no shirt underneath, so only tiny circles of dark brown hair came out above the sweater's V. His shoes were brown-and-white saddle oxfords and he wore them with no socks.

He had already picked out a table and was waiting for me. The table was in a far corner with a view of the entire coffee shop. He motioned for me to sit to his side so I also would have a good view of the entire coffee shop.

"Bogie and I had coffee in a place like this in Lisbon," he said. "It was a mob scene. Every Portuguese with a ballpoint came over for his autograph. I'll bet it's the same for you in this place, right?"

"I'm afraid not," I said. "Lieutenant governors are not that well known outside of their immediate families."

He reached over and slapped me on the top of the hand. "Self-deprecating humor is the best kind, Lewt Guv," he said. "And you've got it. So did Coop."

"Coop?"

"Gary Cooper. We worked on a picture together in London. It was a cameo. All he had to do was pick up a ringing phone on a desk and say, 'Cooper here.' The producer flew him, his wife and five friends to London, all expenses paid, for four weeks so he could say, 'Cooper here.' Plus a fee. The shooting took less than two hours. But that's what it's like in our business. But I'll bet it's interesting in the lieutenant governor's business, too."

31

I decided to get on with my business.

"I just came from the room where you are shooting your movie," I said with all of my lieutenant governor authority. "I am outraged at what I saw, outraged at the kind of movie you are making."

He leaned across the table like he was going to stick his nose in my coffee.

"No visitors are allowed on the sets of my movies," he whispered, as if he were putting out a contract on my life.

"There was some kid there who must have been the director who didn't seem to mind."

"Kid? That young man is none other than R. Peter Rasenberger, the David Lean of tomorrow already on the scene today."

"Oh," I replied.

"David and I almost worked together three times."

Jed Berryhill was no longer looking at me. He was staring at a group of men who had gathered at a long table in the center of the room. There were about ten of them. They were drinking coffee and laughing and carrying on, as grown men friends do over coffee all over Oklahoma and the rest of the normal world.

But Jed Berryhill acted like he had seen a vision. He stood straight up, crooked the index finger of his right hand into a circle with his thumb, and put it to his right eye and looked through the hole toward the men at the table. Like he was Robinson Crusoe. Like he was nuts.

"That's America over there," he said, like he was Christopher Columbus on the bridge of the *Pinta*, the *Niña* or the *Santa María*.

I looked over at the table. There were still about ten men drinking coffee and laughing and carrying on, as grown men friends do over coffee all over Oklahoma and the rest of the normal world.

"Here, look at it," he said to me, holding up his finger-thumb circle to my one good eye.

I looked through the hole.

"That's how it looks to a cameraman," said Berryhill. "Doesn't it make you cry red-white-and-blue tears? Oh, how I wish Spence was here. Oh, how I do wish it."

Spence Tracy, obviously. I decided that the closest this idiot had ever come to Bogie, Coop, Spence or even David Lean, whoever he was, was when he got cheap butter on his fingers from eating popcorn at a movie theater.

We sat back down and I said what I had come to say.

"Your movie is unacceptable to the people of Oklahoma, Mr. Berryhill. You have violated the rules and understandings under which our state movie office assisted you, and thus you must either delete all sex, all profanity and all other things of an objectionable or immoral nature, or cease making the movie."

Jed Berryhill stood straight up and threw his shoulders back.

"Now *I* am outraged, sir!" he shouted. "You have just violated the First Amendment to the Constitution of the United States of America. You are attempting to censor, to violate my freedom of speech and expression. I will not tolerate such unpatriotic behavior."

And he strutted out of the restaurant past the ten men who were still talking and skylarking over coffee. Like he was marching to music from the U.S. Marine Band.

I followed him a few minutes later, after finishing another cup of coffee and having realized—and decided—that I was going to need some special help to solve this problem. It was a job for C. Harry Hayes, director of the Oklahoma Bureau of Investigation.

But first I had to pay a call on Sandra Faye Parsons.

Sandra Faye Parsons was a beautiful white-blonde, vanilla-skinned woman of thirty-five or so who had several degrees in history, including one that made her Dr. Sandra Faye Parsons and a leading expert on the early history of Oklahoma. She was on the staff of the Oklahoma Historical Society, and I had met her when she had been in charge of helping new museums open up in Oklahoma. I loved museums and had been particularly active with a retired rich bus driver friend in the founding of the National Motor Coach Museum in Oklahoma City.

Sandra Faye had called me right after the news had broken about Joe's keynote speech, and said she needed my help on something that had to do with the speech. She had said it related to her new position as director of the Museum of the Cherokee Strip in Enid. So I had said that as coincidence would have it I had to go to Enid in a couple of days and would come by.

So here I was. Her face clicked to highbeam bright the second I said hello to her. She was in an office behind the front desk of the museum.

"Oh, Mack, you came," she said, grabbing my right hand with both of hers just like Jed Berryhill had done.

"How could I have said no to you, Sandra Faye?" I replied.

She said she knew I was a busy man so she would get right to the point of her Call for Help. She asked me to follow her out into the main room of the museum, which was not that big, really. It was smaller than a small high school gymnasium and was made up mostly of little cubicles of old furniture, wagons, photographs, maps and small mementos from the 1883 rush for land in what was called the Cherokee Strip. More than a hundred thousand had come across the border from Kansas at the firing of a gunshot to stake claims. Twenty thousand of them had staked their claims right there in what was now Enid.

Sandra Faye, I am not embarrassed to say, was a pleasure to follow anywhere. She was wearing a rather tight-fitting green knit dress that highlighted her movements in a most attractive way. I am slightly embarrassed to say that I was probably made particularly attentive to her movements by the arousing experience I had had in the Best Western motel room. I was a grown man, but much of that remained a mystery to me.

We stopped in front of several photographs on the wall in the main museum gallery. They were pictures of famous characters from the days of the Cherokee Strip run. There was a shot of a guy named Little Nick De Barscy, a tiny carnival performer who had weighed one and three-quarters pounds when he was born—a birth that had left his mother with a full beard, for reasons medical science had never been able to determine. There was another, of Louis Wilkins, Jr., from nearby Waukomis, who was known as the Waukomis Giant because he stood nine feet, two inches tall, weighed 325 pounds and wore a size 16 glove.

But Sandra Faye had asked me to come because of another man. She pointed to a retouched portrait of a man sitting in a chair. He was wearing a coat, a vest and a small bow tie. His hair was dark and slicked back, as was the thick mustache that came down from under his nose in an almost perfect half-moon. A newspaper was on his lap, and his eyes were staring ahead but not right into the camera. There was something about his eyes that did not look right.

"This is David E. George," said Sandra Faye. "Or at least

that was the name he died under, here in Enid on January 13, 1903. He killed himself. He walked from his room at the Grand Hotel to the Watrous Drug Store nearby, bought a bottle of strychnine, took it back to his room, drank it and died."

How interesting, I thought. But so what? I also thought.

"Right after he died, the word got around—I won't bore you with the details—that this man had claimed to be John Wilkes Booth, the actor who shot President Abraham Lincoln. He had told a man in Texas that he had escaped from a burning tobacco barn in Virginia and that another man had died and been buried as Booth. The people around here knew him only as a kind of bummy housepainter with a drinking problem."

And from there, as Sandra Faye told the story, it got strange.

The undertaker there in Enid had heard the story of the dead man's claims, so instead of burying him he embalmed him with a technique using arsenic that turned this poor man in the photograph into a mummy. Along had come a young man with an entrepreneurial mind who suggested to the undertaker that he dress up the mummy and display it as the man who had claimed to be John Wilkes Booth. Good idea, said the undertaker, so he tied the mummy up in that chair, put the newspaper in its lap and charged people ten cents for a view.

But that was still nowhere near the end of the story.

"Doctors were brought in to examine the body to see if it was possible to determine if he was in fact John Wilkes Booth," said Sandra Faye. "Using information about scars and bone breaks and things like that, some of the doctors said yes, he was in fact John Wilkes Booth. But others said no. After four years of being on display at the funeral home, the body was sold to a man who rented it out to carnivals. It went all over the country, to towns large and small. For a while, promoters offered a thousand dollars to anyone who could prove it really wasn't Booth. The record is silent on whether or not anyone ever collected the money."

"Was it or wasn't it really Booth?" I asked at that moment.

"Well, we still do not know."

"Where is the mummy now?" I asked, realizing as I asked that that was exactly what I was supposed to ask.

"Well, that is the most interesting part of the story," she said. "And why I wanted to see you. We know a man named R. K. Verbeck of Cabbage Corners, Ohio, claims to have bought it for fifteen dollars for his Living Museum of Show Business in the late 1950s. A woman in Philadelphia said she had been holding it as security from a boarder who could not pay his rent. But Mr. Verbeck said when he went to pick it up, in 1958, the rooming house had been demolished in an urban renewal project and the woman and the mummy were nowhere to be found."

I shook my head in amazement.

"We believe there is a very good possibility that the mummy still exists," said Sandra Faye. "Who would throw away a mummy, Mack? It is not the kind of thing you leave outside for the trash man."

I agreed.

"We of the Oklahoma Historical Society and the Museum of the Cherokee Strip believe that mummy belongs here," she said. "I mean, right here. Literally, right here where this picture hangs. We think it would be a terrific drawing card for the museum and thus for interest in the history of our state. Don't you agree?"

I told her I agreed.

"Well, there you have it, Mack. Will you help us?"

"Help you do what?"

"Find the mummy of David E. George, alias John Wilkes Booth."

"How could I do that?"

"Get Governor Hayman to put something about it in his keynote speech. Millions of people all over this country will be watching on televison. What better way to spread the word? All he would have to say is something like, 'Someone out there has in their home, their basement, their attic, their office, a mummy that rightfully belongs in Enid, Oklahoma. Would you please help us find that person and help us return the mummy to Enid?' Something like that. Could you get the governor to say that? Anything at all would be helpful. Please, Mack?"

I told her that was out of the question. "Sandra Faye, please," I said. "Keynote speeches are to sound the alarm for America and the Democratic Party, not for mummy searches."

"I understand," she said, taking my right hand again in both of hers. "Thank you for listening to the story. There are not many important people around who would take the time for such a thing."

I told her to think nothing of it and, shaking my head, went out to find C. Harry Hayes.

C. Harry Hayes was known as the legendary director of the Oklahoma Bureau of Investigation. He was legendary partly because of his reputation for integrity and toughness and partly because he and his friends, of which I was the best, like to make up stories about him. We were friends by

accident, because normally the head of the OBI and the lieutenant governor would have little to say to one another, other
than an occasional hello at a party or luncheon. But a few
years ago, Buffalo Joe and circumstances had thrown us together on a project. We had found that we liked and trusted
each other, and before we knew it, we were friends with an
interest in helping each other out in times of need. Like now.

"I need this movie guy to understand it is in our power
to put him out of business," I said of my current need, after
I explained to C. what I had found at the Enid motel.

"You mean, Mr. Lieutenant Governor, that you want me
to use the force of law enforcement and justice to harass a
private citizen."

"Yes, Mr. Director, a citizen of California, not of Oklahoma."

C. always dressed in gray, because, he said, it made everything so much easier. He never had to waste time thinking
about what to put on in the morning or what color clothes
to buy at Sears, his favorite shopping place. Today he had
on a dark gray sport coat and light gray slacks, and a gray-
and-black tie on top of his white shirt. We were sitting side
by side in the backseat of his OBI command car, a black
Lincoln Continental that was equipped with machine guns,
tear-gas canisters, portable megaphones and other things
needed to cope with flood, famine, riot, robbery and insur-
rection on Oklahoma soil. I always sat on the left so I could
see him better with my one eye, the right one, and he could
hear me with his one ear, the left one. He had lost his ear in
a pistol-range accident when he was a rookie cop. I had lost
my eye in a kick-the-can-game accident when I was a kid.

"Everything's got to be kept tight," I said. "I want him to
know we—the state, me—are behind it, but we obviously

have got to make sure he can't make any police-state or First Amendment hay if it goes sour."

"Obviously," said C.

"We also are not keen on having to explain how Oompah, on behalf of the State of Oklahoma, helped some perverts make a porno flick at a Best Western in Enid," I said.

"That's also an obviously," said C.

He took a bite of his barbecued pork on a sesame bun sandwich. We had just gone through the drive-thru at the Flying Pig–Northwest on 63rd. C.'s idea of a good time was to eat a fast-food lunch while riding around Oklahoma City in the backseat of his car. We did it a couple of times a month. I had set this one up for two days after I returned from Enid.

At first we had always had either Big Macs or Whoppers, but after a while C. decided to move us on to pizza and now to barbecue.

He saved up stories for me from the annals of Oklahoma crime. Today he had one about a case of superswift justice. A WM-24 (white male, twenty-four years old) had broken into a substantial house outside Nowata while the residents had been away shopping in Claremore. He had loaded up his purple Chevy pickup with a TV, an electric blender and a portable air-conditioning window unit, and then gone back inside for more. He had taken two shotguns, a .38-caliber pistol and a bow-and-arrow set from a sitting room on the second floor.

"The man was in a hurry and he was a fool," C. said. "He tried to carry all those weapons at the same time. So you can guess what happened.

I couldn't.

"He tripped coming down the stairs, and one of the arrows went right through his gut. They found him down the road in his purple pickup all bled to death. The woman who owns the house is a big ear-splitting Baptist. She swears God punished the perpetrator right there on the spot to save the State of Oklahoma the trouble and expense."

"Hard to argue otherwise, I guess."

"Precisely," said C., who used the word "precisely" a lot.

After a while we finished lunch and were back at the capitol parking lot.

"I'm thinking we ought to switch to Chinese," C. said as we did our good-byes. "There's a dandy-looking Oklahoma Nanking Express with a drive-thru over near the fairgrounds."

"I hate Chinese food," I said.

"It'll grow on you," C. said.

Two nights later, Jackie and I went to dinner with Ron Hammerschmidt, president of Continental Trailways. We had just sat down with him at a corner table in the dining room of the Park Plaza Hotel, when I asked him:

"How did you travel from Dallas to Oklahoma City today?"

"Via Continental Trailways, the easiest travel on earth, to the next town or across America," he said, in the singsong of a radio commercial.

"See," I said to Jackie. "I told you real bus people really do ride buses. She was willing to bet money you flew up here."

"Seldom a week goes by that I am not on one of our buses somewhere," said Ron. "Always unannounced, always to see how we're doing."

"I do the same thing with my stores," Jackie said. "Just pull into one and see how I am treated and served. Our employees call them Jackie Attacks."

"Ours call my trips Ron Runs."

Ron Hammerschmidt was tall and skinny and loose-boned like a puppet. His hair was red and curly and his face was full of freckles. Only around his eyes, which were Greyhound blue, did he show any age. I guessed him to be about forty-five years old.

And he talked in sheets. In storms. Words poured out of his mouth. And poured out of his mouth. Like he was being paid by the word to talk. With some extra thrown in he could keep everyone else from talking, too. It wasn't speechy. In fact, he spoke quietly and informally. And it was interesting and important. It was just that he didn't stop.

We were barely into our salads—I shared with Jackie a Caesar without the anchovies, which I still hated—when he began his presentation, his first storm. "I have come," he said, "to discuss the survival of Continental Trailways and the entire intercity bus industry. Unless something is done, and done fast, it is not going to be here much longer. At least not very much of it. The combination of the cheap car and the cheap airliner has turned us into the transportation system of last resort. All that is left for us are the poor, the elderly and the sick. Those with no other choice. There are not going to be enough of those people around much longer to keep us and Greyhound and all the other smaller companies in business. We are doomed. We are buggy whips. Say "bus" to the average Oklahoman, and what comes to his mind? I'll tell you: misery, dirty restrooms, lost baggage, sleeping drunks. We are doomed unless we move, and move fast. Unless we begin to think with our heads and our imaginations. Unless we come to grips with the fact that the choice is between a new-age future or a no future. I kept looking around for that someone who was going to step in and save us with that new-age future, but I can't find anybody. Not an anybody any-where. So I decided to do it myself. I am my own last resort. Either I do it or I preside over the end of an industry I love, an industry that is essential to America, even though America does not know it."

Jackie and I finished our salad, and the waiter brought our main courses after Ron, who had taken only one bite of his tossed salad with blue cheese dressing, motioned that he was through, too. He did not take his eyes off us. He did not allow a pause that was long enough to ask a question or make a comment.

"There was a time when little boys wanted to grow up to be bus drivers. There was a time when the college student and the businessman and the nurse and the lawyer and the teacher also rode on our buses. There was a time when we were part of the transportation consciousness of this nation. Let me give you one number. Just one number. Just one. And the number is One. One percent. One-point-two percent, to be precise. One-point-two percent of the traveling between cities and towns in this country now is done on buses. One-point-two percent! And it goes down every year. It won't be long before we're at one-one and then a naked one. And then we're into point-ninety-nine. And on down and down to point-nothing and oblivion. So what do we do? What does somebody like me looking for the answer do? Where does he look? Does it make sense to try to compete with the automobile? No. Not as long as there is cheap gasoline avail-able. About the only way we could do something about the automobile is to start a war in the Middle East and keep it going for years. How about that for a solution? Instead of buying new buses and building new terminals and advertising, we in the bus business finance and foment war and disruption in places like Saudi Arabia, Kuwait and Iran. How about that?"

How about that?

"Does it make any sense to try to compete with the airlines? How? It took four hours and five minutes for the bus to take me up here from Dallas just now. On the plane, it's forty-five minutes. Four hours and five minutes versus forty-five minutes. Do you know what the difference in fare is? We charge forty-five dollars. They charge fifty-five. Only a fool or somebody scared to death of flying would ride a bus instead of a plane. Am I not right? You bet I am right. And there are not enough fools and somebodies scared to death in the United States of America to keep our buses in passengers. So forget trying to compete with airlines. We can't do it. It is pointless to try.

"So where does that leave us? It leaves us with only one alternative. Do something different. Get out of the failing business we are now in and create a new one. I have an idea for creating a new business that would involve your JackieMarts with our bus company as two of three parts to a new-age future. The third part would be National Parcel Delivery Service."

He took the sugar bowl and placed it in front of him. "This is a JackieMart." He took the saltshaker in his left hand. "This is a Continental Trailways bus." He took the pepper shaker in his right hand. "This is a National Parcel Delivery Service truck." He put them both down in front of the sugar bowl. He picked up the single rose in a slim crystal vase. "This is an American people. He and she lives in a town or a neighborhood served by a JackieMart. What if it were possible to also catch the bus to Houston or Oklahoma City or wherever at the JackieMart? And ship or receive a package?" He picked up the two shakers. "What if the bus and the truck became one? Right now this bus and this truck are traveling down the same roads, one carrying the people, the other delivering packages. What if we built a vehicle that was half bus and half truck? What if they made the JackieMarts their headquarters? What if we operated fleets of small vans from those JackieMarts, that went on call to pick up people or their packages for the bus? What if we created a whole new one-stop service industry combining several services in a way that was mutually beneficial to all?"

It took a few seconds for me to realize Ron had stopped talking.

He had ordered some kind of veal dish. He was cutting little bits of veal into even smaller bits. Jackie and I were so used to not talking that neither of us said a word. We just watched him cut his veal. I was nearly through with my linguine-with-mushroom-sauce main course. She was finished with her smoked salmon and broccoli.

He took two bites of veal. There were only a few other patrons in the restaurant and we were over in a corner, so there was no noise. Except for the sound of his cutting and chewing.

He began again.

"Please, do not give me your reaction tonight," he said directly to Jackie. "Think it over. I will contact you in a day or two. I will then set up a meeting among the three of us. Douglas Kendall Smith has heard what you have heard. I had dinner with him in Atlanta two nights ago. I plan to call him for his reaction tomorrow. Even if it is favorable and yours is favorable, obviously we have just begun. What kind of relationship should it be? Do we start small with some experimental arrangements, or do we go all the way? Do we remain independent from each other, or do we form a new company? If so, how do we distribute the ownership and control? What do we call our creation? Where will our head-quarters be? What will our logo be? What about our unions? When do we tell Wall Street? The press? How do we keep our respective competitors, Greyhound, UPS and 7-Eleven, from stealing our idea and doing it first?"

Jackie and I did as we were told. We did not react. We all three skipped dessert, but over coffee talked mostly about the coming presidential election and the Democratic convention and whom Senator Griffin might choose as his running mate. Senator Griffin was Daniel Michael Griffin of New Jersey. He had already wrapped up the presidential nomination in the primaries and caucuses. The convention was merely a formality now.

Hammerschmidt said he had followed the primary campaign very closely and agreed all the way through with what Art Minow said in his column. Minow was a famous syndicated columnist, but I seldom read him because he wasn't in *The Daily Oklahoman* or *Oklahoma City Times*. Neither of the Tulsa papers ran him, either. Only Enid and Muskogee did, and I did not read those papers regularly. I had seen him on television, on the Sunday interview programs and those things on Saturday night where people like Minow mostly just yell at each other. Minow had also spoken at a convention of one of the many groups Jackie belonged to. I think it was the Southwestern Association of Convenience Store Operators. I had also heard him talk three years before at the fall meeting of the National Association of Lieutenant Governors in Lake Charles, Louisiana. NALG had paid him $17,500 for making the hourlong speech. I knew that because I happened to be on the meeting's arrangements subcommittee that year.

46

It stunned me to learn that anybody got paid that kind of money to make a speech. Any kind of speech about anything to anybody.

"Minow says Griffin was liberal enough to get the Democratic nomination, because only that kind can. But he's too liberal to win the election, because only nonliberals can."

I said hopeful things about Joe Hayman and the possibility of his being on the ticket as balance.

Ron Hammerschmidt said that would be just great. "If he got elected, then maybe he could help us take over the post offices, too."

"Take over the post offices?" said Jackie with some alarm.

"Think about it," said Hammerschmidt. "The ultimate privatization. We—this new arrangment of ours—contracts with the government to deliver the mail. JackieMarts double as post offices, particularly in the small towns. Our combination truck-buses also become mail trucks. Think about it. It's good for the government, it's good for us."

He insisted on picking up the check, and Jackie and I let him.

We drove home shaking our heads and wondering if this was the way Sears and Roebuck, Procter and Gamble, and all the others got together to create American history's great and exciting new ventures of private enterprise.

3
. . .
COW BABY

The week-from-today deadline Joe had given Cow Cowell
came and went without a speech or a word from Cow Cowell.
Joe said I should go down to Pauls Valley and find out what
was going on. "Go there in my name and find out what in
the hell is going on," were his exact words. He said both the
Democratic National Committee people and the Griffin campaign had to see it and approve it ahead of time. Time was
wasting.

Pauls Valley was only an hour south on I-35, so the next
morning I went there in my dark blue Buick Skylark. It took
only one stop at one Shell station to find out where Cow lived
and, more important, where he was now. The guy at the
station said Cow was always at Armbruster's Diner at this
time of morning. Always. Armbruster's was in the middle of
downtown and had at one time been the depot for the old
All-American Bus Lines that had gone through the town on
the Oklahoma City–Dallas leg of its legendary New York–

48

Los Angeles route. It was legendary because the passengers had been given free pillows and meals, and had been paid a penny a minute for every minute over thirty that the bus was late. Armbruster's was legendary for its Christmas fruitcakes. It sold thousands of them every year to people who called and wrote in their orders from all over the world. I never cared for fruitcakes of any kind myself, but that was something I kept to myself, particularly when I was in Pauls Valley and at Armbruster's.

I had never laid my one good eye on Cow Cowell before, but a no-eyed man could have spotted him. He was short and bald. What little hair he had was almost snow-white, and it grew in tangled messes around his mouth in what I guess was an attempt at a handlebar mustache and a Santa Claus beard. I knew bald people liked to compensate for having no hair on their head by growing a lot everywhere else, but Cow Cowell had gone too far. I could barely see that under all that hair his face was round like a basketball and about the same color, a Wilson's Sporting Goods regulation orangy-brown.

He was sitting at the counter talking to a man on his left and the waitress behind the counter. The morning breakfast rush was over, and now it was strictly coffee-breakers and loafers.

I took the empty stool next to him and introduced myself.

"You came for the speech, I guess?" Cow Cowell said immediately.

"You win the prize with that guess, Mr. Cowell," I replied.

"Good. It's about time. Cup of coffee?"

I smiled, and the waitress, a lovely young blonde who reminded me of a shampoo commercial, brought me coffee and a little white porcelain pitcher of cream.

49

"How do you like being Number Two to a turkey like Hayman?" Cow said.

"That man you call a turkey may end up vice-president of the United States."

Cow Cowell broke into a hairy little-boy grin. Like he had just been told he could have the three cookies and the root beer float after all.

"Think about that for a moment. Think about Buffalo Joe Hayman's heart beating up there in Washington just a skip and a jump away from having his finger on the button that could destroy the world. Think about it." Cow Cowell made sounds like a heart beating. "Buburoom, buburoom, buburoom." Then they got louder. Like a bomb exploding. "Baarroom! Baarroom! Baarroom!"

"Where's the speech?" I said.

He gave me the grin again. And tapped a finger to his head. "It's all written right up there."

"It's not on paper?"

"Not yet."

"When?"

"Maybe tomorrow."

"Maybe right now, you mean."

"No way, Mr. Lieutenant Governor."

"Right now, Mr. Cowell."

"Call me Cow. Cow as in moooo."

"Call me Mack. Mack as in truck."

We left Armbruster's in separate cars. I was to follow him to his place, where, despite his protests, we would sit down at his typewriter and bang it out. His car was actually a very old four-seater jeep that had been painted bright sunflower yellow. I followed him easily for five or six blocks east across the Santa Fe tracks and out of the business district. We came to an open field and suddenly he gunned it and made a hard turn up over the curb and across the field. There was a slight incline, and he disappeared on the other side while I watched helplessly. There was no way my Buick could make it across that open field.

It took me twenty minutes to find him and his place. And by that time I had decided that Cow as in Moooo was much, much more trouble than he could ever, ever be worth. It wouldn't matter if he could write another Gettysburg Address.

His place was an old hardware store on the opposite side of town. I mean a real old hardware store. Walking through the front door was like walking into a hardware store in the 1940s. There were old tools on racks, nails and screws in barrels, rubber hoses and belts on pegs, plus sink stoppers, faucets, axe handles, string, barbed wire, chain of all widths and lengths, washtubs and washboards displayed around. There were big stand-up cardboard posters on the counters advertising paint and varnish. One wall was nothing but little wooden drawers with white porcelain pulls. Like a giant chest of drawers. A sample of what was in each drawer was hanging on the outside. Wrenches, nuts, bolts, chisels, clamps, caps— everything was there. The only thing out of sync was the odor. It smelled of burning alfalfa rather than machine oil and metal like most hardware stores.

Cow was standing just inside, waiting for me. Grinning.

"What is this?" I said, looking around in awe. Real awe.

"The man who owned it dropped dead one afternoon in here twenty-seven years ago." He pointed to a spot near a huge brass cash register. "He was picking up a cardboard box of wood screws about there where you are. He dropped the box, fell to his knees, then on his face, and never took another breath. His wife locked the door and left it the way it was that afternoon. Then four years ago she died and her kids sold it to me." He pointed upward. There was a balcony that went around three sides of the store. "I live up there."

"It's like a museum. Or a place to make a movie about a hardware store," I said. I regret to say that I could not help but imagine what Melody Anderson and that guy would look like doing their awful things over there on the floor by the cash register while David E. George, alias John Wilkes Booth, watched from his chair.

"I haven't touched a thing," Cow said.

Then I regained my senses. I did not come all this way to Pauls Valley to have idle chitchat with this idiot.

"What was your little over-hill-and-dale hide-and-seek game all about?" I said without humor.

"I wanted to do some picking up upstairs before you came."

"You are a weird person, Mr. Moooo."

"So maybe are you, Mr. Truck."

What he was looking for, he said, was paper. Something to type on. He said he had a Smith Corona typewriter that was ancient, upright and in working order. But there was no typing paper because this was a hardware store not a stationery store.

He was interrupted by a very loud, very feminine screech: "Cow baby? Who are you talking to?"

It came from up and back. The same place the alfalfa smell was coming from.

"It's the lieutenant governor of Oklahoma, sweetheart!" Cowell screeched back.

"I've never seen a lieutenant governor before, Cow Baby," the feminine voice answered. I figured her to be about twenty and from Arkansas and not too bright.

"They look like governors, except they only have one eye instead of two."

And suddenly I lost my patience.

"Mr. Cowell, let me give it to you straight. There is a whole lot riding on this speech. A lot more than you. You have until this time tomorrow to have it done." I looked down at my wristwatch. "Have it done and on my desk in Oklahoma City by eleven-oh-seven in the A.M., or else!"

"Or else what?"

"I'll have you arrested."

"For what?"

"I've got until eleven-oh-seven in the A.M. to figure that out."

My lost patience was as much with Buffalo Joe as it was with this idiot Cow. How in the world Joe could turn over something as important as his whole future political life to this deadbeat immoral creep was more than I could understand.

When I was at the door it dawned on me that it was not burning alfalfa I was smelling. It was probably something C. and his friends in law enforcement called an Illegal Substance. I had never personally smelled the odor of such a thing, but it was worth the gamble.

"I think I have figured out something to arrest you for," I said with a long, noisy, exaggerated sniff. And no grin. "How about possession of marijuana? A jury of your peers here in God-fearing Pauls Valley might give you life for that, Mr. Mooo."

"See you at eleven-oh-seven in the A.M., Mr. Truck," he said.

Of course, 11:07 came and went without a sign of Cow Cowell. Of course. It was stupid even to dream that he would show up. I was already dreading having to go into Joe and tell him there was no speech. And there would never, ever be a speech if it was left to the creep in Pauls Valley.

I decided to give Cowell a little something to remember me by. I knew about what a lot of the young people and professors in places like California and Massachusetts thought about marijuana. But this was Oklahoma, and I had taken an oath as lieutentant governor to ensure that the laws of the state were faithfully executed. That included drug laws.

I got C. on the phone. "First, what is new on the movie deal?" I asked.

"You should be hearing from the man in question very shortly. What's second?"

"I have a crime to report," I said.

"Call your local police," he said.

"This is a crime that knows no borders, no races, no creeds, no classes."

"If you're talking about sex or speeding, call the highway patrol."

"I'm talking about drugs, about Illegal Substances."

"Pot?"

"Yes."

"You been down at OU?"

"I've been down to Pauls Valley. I smelled it myself. The criminal's name is Marvin Cowell. They call him ..."

"Cow. They call him Cow. I'd be surprised if he was not in the possession of an Illegal Substance."

"I want him arrested."

"Hey, Mack, Cow's okay."

"I want him arrested, C. Possession of marijuana is a serious criminal offense in this state, as I certainly do not need to tell you of all people."

"What's the problem, Mack? Cow just writes things. He

wrote a poem once about Oklahoma truck drivers talking on CB radios that was the funniest thing I ever saw. He had a guy on there who talked in nothing but Bible verses. If you asked him where the next McDonald's was on I-40, he'd tell you something from Isaiah 8:12 or some such that, if you listened carefully and knew your Bible, would take you right to the front driveway of a McDonald's. I remember one line about . . ."

"He's in violation of the laws of the State of Oklahoma, which you are responsible for enforcing."

"He's also a kind of cousin-in-law of Will Rogers's, Mack. Nobody knows much about it, but Cow's ex-wife's second cousin was the grandson of Will Rogers's aunt. If you and The Chip want a headline about a Will Rogers kin being arrested in a drug bust on orders from on high, this close to the Democratic National Convention, fine. Wasn't Will Rogers kind of the unofficial mascot of the national Democratic Party there for a while? I am only here to serve, of course." "The Chip" was his private nickname for Buffalo Joe. It derived from "buffalo chip," as in buffalo dung.

It was eleven-forty and there was noise at my office door. Janice Alice Montgomery, my secretary, was trying to hold back a man from entering unannounced. It was Cow. He had a sheaf of eight-by-ten white typing paper in his right hand.

"Cancel the arrest order, Mr. OBI Director," I said into the phone. "I think it was probably alfalfa I smelled after all."

"Whatever you say, Mr. Lieutenant Governor."

I immediately took Cow and the speech and hand-delivered both to Joe, who took the manuscript in his two hands like he was weighing gold on the county scales.

"It feels right, Cow," Joe said. "It feels just right. How much do I owe you?"

"Nothing, Joe," Cow said. We were all three standing in front of Joe's desk. The delivery ceremony seemed too important to be conducted sitting down. "This one's on me."

"Oh no, Cow. I couldn't let you do that."

"I consider it an honor just to be involved in this important part of Oklahoma history. Boomer Sooner and Crown Oklahoma, Joe."

"Boomer Sooner" was the name of the fight song of the University of Oklahoma Sooners. "Crown Oklahoma" was a slogan Joe had invented a few years back for a campaign he had launched to finally put a dome on our domeless capitol building in Oklahoma City. The original plans had included a dome, but the state had run out of money when the capitol was being built in 1915 and so the dome had never gotten on it. Joe's attention had eventually gone on to other things and nothing had ever come of it, but for a while he had us all going around saying "Crown Oklahoma" to each other. The whole campaign had been brought back to life recently by an Oklahoma City lady who still thought it was a good idea. She and an architect cooked up a scheme to finance it with a big plaza of bricks down in front of the capitol on the south side. Each brick would cost $250, and for it the contributor got his or her name or some other his or her name of his or her choice on it. They figured forty thousand bricks at $250 a piece would raise the money for the dome, plus cover the cost of bricking the plaza.

I watched Cow Cowell's hairy basketball face for the sign of a smile. A smart-mouth smile. A snide smile. I didn't see anything like that, but I was still suspicious. Cow Cowell was not the Boomer Sooner or Crown Oklahoma type. He also did not strike me as a man who was prone to writing political speeches for free. The whole thing made me uneasy.

I was later to wish very much that I had acted on my uneasiness.

Coop's and Spence's and Jimmy's friend Jed Berryhill, producer of *Oklahoma Parts*, was waiting for me back at my office. He would not look at me and he would not sit down. Dressed again in a sweater with no shirt, shoes with no socks, and all the rest, he started pacing back and forth across the office and talking like he was a very uptight wind-up talking doll on the verge of blowing its parts all over the room.

"The next afternoon after you left that motel, two thugs in dark suits came by and said they were asbestos inspectors from the State of Oklahoma. They declared that motel room where we were shooting to be a killer room. They put up a sign on the door condemning it and forced us to evacuate. We moved to another room. Another thug, in a fireman's suit, showed up to say it did not meet the fire code. We decided to move from the Best Western to a Holiday Inn. We got our gear packed into our U-Haul trucks, and four cops drove up. Our vehicles were declared mechanically in violation of Oklahoma safety inspection regulations. Our driver's driver's license was declared invalid because it said he was five feet nine and any fool could tell by looking he was a least five-ten or maybe even five-ten and a half."

He stopped, took a breath, glanced at me with a killer look and continued. I kept a straight face and said nothing.

"We tried to rent new trucks. Ryder turned us down on credit grounds. So did Avis and Budget and Hertz and several others. We finally got a company named Second Hand Wheels to rent us a pair of old International pickups. Two of our crew members were picked up that night coming out of the Holiday Inn bar, on public drunkenness charges. They were not drunk and all they were doing was walking back to their rooms. A justice of the peace refused them bail, so they had to spend the night in jail. The next morning a man and a woman, both dressed in phony-looking white coats, came to the Holiday Inn. They identified themselves as agents with the Oklahoma State Venereal Disease Control Board. They kept saying 'OSVDCB' like they were Efrem Zimbalist, Jr., of the FBI. They forced our two stars, Scott and Melody, to pee in bottles and undergo hands-on inspections of their private parts."

I had to look away to keep from breaking up. If there had been a window in my office, I would have looked out it and sent C. some kind of psychic-wave message. A message of, "Come on, C.!"

"They declared both Scott and Melody to be PCs. Potential carriers," Jed Berryhill went on. "They took them off to a hospital emergency room and forced them to take penicillin tablets and then ordered them held overnight for observation. The next day two vice detectives from the Enid Police Department came to inquire if it was true a minor female was being forced to have what they called 'perverted sex' with an older man. They said it was against Oklahoma law for a minor female to have perverted sex with an older man. They insisted on stationing a detective in the room during the shooting to monitor the situation."

He stopped walking and talking. He seemed out of steam, out of breath. The toy had finally wound down.

He held his hands up in the air above his head. "I surrender, Lewt Guv. You and your thugs win. I have one-point-five mil of other people's money in this picture. I lose it, I lose a piece of my ass."

"There's no need to be coarse, Mr. Berryhill," I said, in a most official OSVDCB manner.

"You have used the official cloak of your office and of the State of Oklahoma to harass me, and you say, 'No need to be coarse.' There is a lot of famous dialogue that has already been written for a situation like this. But I choose not to speak it. Just tell me, please, how we can make a deal?"

I was ready. I said: "Change the name of the movie."

"To what?"

"To *Arkansas Parts*. *New Mexico Parts*. Something like that. Anything but *Kansas Parts*."

"Done. What's your problem with Kansas, just so I'll know?"

"I was born in Kansas. Also, do not mention Oklahoma or our film office in any credits or press statements or anything else."

"Done."

I stood and extended my hand to him. He pulled himself to his feet but did not take my hand.

"I'm going to put you in a movie someday, Lewt Guv. It's going to be a horror story about the First Amendment to the Constitution of the United States, about abuse of official power that will make Watergate look like peanuts."

"I'd be honored to play myself, sir. Thank you."

Joe changed the course of my history the next morning.

I went around to tell him that I had solved the Movie Thing, but I never got a chance to. I found him standing in front of his closed office window with his back to the door, speaking at top and dramatic volume toward downtown Oklahoma City.

He must have seen my reflection in the window, because he stopped before I could pick up on anything he said other than, "...America of today is like America of yesterday, which is like America of tomorrow..."

"It is a fine speech, Mack," he said. "All of the parties in the party have cleared it. Griffin's people included. That's Senator Daniel Michael Griffin, the man who may choose the next vice-president of the United States. A fine speech, Mack. Cow may be a screwball weirdo fruitcake dopehead liberal, but he writes a national speech. A national speech."

Then Joe walked out from behind his desk and came right up to me. He was so close I could tell he had had orange marmalade on his wheat toast for breakfast. He grabbed my right hand in both of his, much like Jed Berryhill, the movie man, had done the first time I met him. And Sandra Faye Parsons had done an hour or so later.

A tear formed down in the corner of Joe's right eye.

"I take your right hand, Mack, because you are my right hand, Mack. I must have you there with me. I mean New York. I want you in New York. I want you at that convention."

"Can both of us be gone from the state at the same time? What does the Constitution say?"

"I am sure it says the First Man of Oklahoma has a right to have the Second Man of Oklahoma with him at times of great import to the State of Oklahoma whenever and wherever he so desires. I so desire. Get ready, Mack. Get ready for the time of your life, Second Man."

Get ready for the time of your life, Second Man.

4
. . .

THE SPIRIT
OF JOE HAYMAN

The plane was a DC-9. Its real name was *The Spirit of Cal Blackwell*, but it had been temporarily renamed *The Spirit of Joe Hayman* for the flight to New York City. Cal Blackwell was what the out-of-state papers called an Eccentric Oklahoma Oil and Gas Millionaire. He had gone to Northwestern Oklahoma State with Joe, and they had remained close personal and political friends in spite of Cal's reputation as a weirdo. Also in spite of Cal's near miss with prison. He had pleaded guilty and gotten five years' probation for drilling wells that slanted over from his oilless land to tap into his neighbor's producing wells. But that had been several years before and was seldom mentioned, if remembered. Most of the weirdo reputation came from his owning the finest collection of blue 1948 Packards in the world. They were parked bumper to bumper in huge circles in a glass-covered round arena in the center of his ten-thousand-acre ranch between Elk City and Woodward in western Oklahoma.

"How many of those Packards do you have now?" I asked Cal, just making conversation.

"One hundred and forty-seven and still counting," Cal replied.

We were seated in cushy leather swivel chairs across from one another in the plane's main compartment, which was a replica of the lobby of the Park Plaza, the best hotel in Oklahoma City. Joe was back in one of the bedrooms going over that speech of his. For the millionth time. Joe's wife, Jill, was reading a magazine about homes and gardens, and his two teenage sons were up watching the pilots fly the plane.

Jill Hayman was somebody I did not see that much or know that well. She and Joe had met after he was already in politics. She had been a high school history and civics teacher in Weatherford. Joe, who was a twenty-nine-year-old member of the Oklahoma House, had come to the school for "Living Oklahoma Government Day." She had been assigned to meet him at the front door of the school when he arrived, escort him around and then introduce him to the student body during an assembly. Joe's version of the story was: "I took one look at that magnificent woman and I said to God in Heaven, 'Please, dear Lord, let me have her. Let me take her from this place to wherever Your light leads us.' He answered my prayer that very night. When I drove out of Weatherford on Highway Sixty-six back toward Oklahoma City, that magnificent woman was sitting up there in the front seat with me. Right there with me that very night. Don't tell me God does not live and God does not do the work that needs to be done. It was enough to turn me into a religious fanatic. I am serious, Mack. Think about that kind of thing happening. Pray for something at eleven-fifteen A.M., and before eleven-fifteen P.M. that very same day, there you are with the answer to that prayer sitting right there in the front seat with you."

Nobody, including me I am sorry to say, ever understood the attraction. Joe called her his Magnificent Woman, which may have been his loving way of saying she was an extremely large woman in every respect. Large legs, large middle section, large upper torso, and large in the head, nose and ears, large even in voice. She spoke in an opera singer kind of way. Deep, almost like a man who sang tenor. Her hair was always short and dyed. Sometimes it was blond, then it was red, then black, and so on. Somebody who saw her a lot more than I did figured she changed the color of her hair an average of nine times each calendar year. The important thing was that she adored Joe and did not truck with anyone who did not also adore him. She was supposed to be brilliant, and maybe she was, but to be quite honest I had not talked to her enough to know for sure. "It's a tie," was the way Jackie put it. "I look at her and I can't see what in the world he sees in her, and then I look at him and say the same thing about him. Ties go to the winner, but who is the winner in this case?" C.'s nickname for her was "The Block." So, as a couple, Joe and Jill were The Chip and The Block. To C. Only to C.

The main public thing about her was her singing of "God Bless America": she was known informally as the Kate Smith of western Oklahoma for the way she sang "God Bless America." In the early days, she had opened or closed most of Joe's political rallies by singing it. She still did it on special occasions, like state Democratic conventions, Oklahoma Hall of Fame dinners and statewide broadcasts of the state finals in basketball and track and field. Joe had tried to get them to let her sing it at Madison Square Garden right after his keynote speech, but they, the officials of the national Democratic Party, would not agree. I had heard her do it eight or nine times, and to my ear she was great. Almost as good as the great Kate Smith herself. Jill's physical attributes obviously helped the comparison along. What was interesting was that I never heard of Jill's ever singing any song but "God Bless America."

She and I had not exchanged ten words since we all met up at the airport in Oklahoma City. I made no attempt to talk to her now. What was I going to say? "Hey, Jill, sorry to hear they won't let you sing 'God Bless America' at Madison Square Garden"?

"Are you still looking for them?" I asked Cal, staying with our conversation about his Packards.

"All the time. I've got one spotted in a junkyard outside Yuma, Arizona, as we speak. Needs a motor, a crankshaft, a rear end, windows and a dash, but we'll make do."

Cal was the most relaxed man in his forties I had ever known. Maybe it was his almost having gone to jail that kept him loose. Whatever. He wore mostly spit-shined black cowboy boots, unstarched blue jeans and tan shirts with military loops on each shoulder like the kind U.S. Army Air Corps pilots wore in World War II. Never once did I hear him raise his quiet, fudgy voice. His tanned face always seemed to have one of those I-have-something-you-don't grins on it. At first I figured it was just because he was rich, that what he had that the rest of us didn't have was money. But it was something else. Maybe it was being able to bring himself to collect blue 1948 Packards.

"I forget now how you got to collecting those Packards," I said.

"My dad was a wildcatter. He would make lots of money all of a sudden and then lose it all of a sudden. When he was flush, we lived like lions. When he was down, we lived like mice. His favorite car was a Packard. A blue 1948 Packard. He bought it new the first time he made some money. It had leather seats like these, and it had a rear window that went up. All you did was press a button on the dash. White side-walls all the way to the tread. A glass knob on the gearshift lever that resembled a gigantic jewel from a ring. Every time his luck ran out, he sold that car, and then bought it back a few weeks or months later when things picked up again. He must have bought and sold it ten times. Then he was dying of lung cancer. He said to me, Cal, I want you to have that car. He said he was willing it to me. I was sixteen at the time, so I was old enough and smart enough to know he was in a down time right then, which meant he didn't have that Pack-ard. But I thanked him and cried about it anyhow. Then right before he died, he said, Cal, go out there and work hard and right, so you can buy every blue 1948 Packard in the world.

"So I did."

A young black man in a white coat brought us drinks. All I wanted was a Pepsi. Cal drank mostly milk and bourbon. Separately. The young man brought him a glass of each.

"You collect anything like Packards, Mack?" Cal asked.

"No. I have a few old bus depot signs, things like that. Nothing like Packards."

"Bus depot signs? And people think collecting old Packards is a bit Tulsa." Cal shared Joe's dislike for cities, particularly Tulsa. He used "Tulsa" as a synonym for "crazy." "I bought those Packards because I wanted to. It was for pure pleasure, not for business. But they are worth a fortune now. A real fortune. Look at your watch."

I looked down at my wristwatch.

"Okay, one, two, three, four, five. Five seconds just went by. Right?"

"That's right, Cal."

"In those five seconds the value of my one hundred forty-seven Packards went up five hundred dollars. Every five seconds means five hundred more dollars of worth for those cars. You'd be well advised to collect cars as an investment, if for no other reason. Forget oil and cattle and stocks and bonds and all of that crap. Go into cars. Pick you a particular make, model and year, like I did. It doesn't have to be anything old or fancy. Something they're selling as used or junk now. Something like a 'sixty-five white Chevy Impala, say. Just start picking them and parking them. Someday they'll be your future. Like a well that produces forever. That's for sure, Mack. For sure."

"Thanks, Cal. I'll surely think about it."

"How are you fixed for money now?"

I reached for my billfold to see how much I had.

"No, Mack. I mean overall. Have you got a nest egg somewhere?"

"My wife's drive-thru grocery business is growing and thriving. There's even some major merger-and-expansion talk under way that I can't talk about. . . ."

"Sorry she couldn't go to New York with us."

"Me, too." Jackie had wanted to, but Joe's invitation had come too late. She was already booked to chair the annual meeting of the Southwest Conference of Women Business Owners at Lake Murray, down by Ardmore. Also, Hammerschmidt the Trailways man had asked her to stay close to home in case something hot came up on The Deal that needed quick action.

Cal said, "Her things really don't count. I mean you."

"I have nothing of my own to really speak of. Actually, I have nothing at all."

"Pick a make, model and year, and go, Mack. It could change your life."

I had no expectations about going to New York City, because I had never expected that I would ever be going to New York City. It was a place in movies and books and songs and television news, a place about which I had had no dreams or longings, boyhood or grown-up. It might as well have been on Mars or in France, for all it mattered to me, one way or another. I had come through the airport named for John F. Kennedy there once, on a trip to France, and that was as close as I figured I would ever get.

So when *The Spirit of Joe Hayman* landed at Kennedy Airport, I was in a nonexcited, mostly uncurious state about where we were. It was the national convention of my party and Joe's moment in the sun that I had come to witness. Not New York City.

Then we got into a very long gray limousine. It had dark-sunglasses glass windows, a color TV set, stereo, a bar, eight or nine national magazines, and individual air-conditioning spigots. And a telephone. I had been in limousines before in Oklahoma, but nothing as long and elaborate as this.

Then we got on a freeway for the drive into the main part of town, where our hotel was. Everything was yellow, as far as the eye could see. Yellow taxicabs in all the lanes, moving as fast as race cars on a western Oklahoma drag strip. Most of their drivers were either honking their horns or exhibiting obscene gestures to each other and their fellow motorists. I could not understand why everybody seemed so mad. And where in the world were they all going now?

Then we got to the hotel, the Claremont. My room was a suite as large as most regular nonmillionaire houses in Oklahoma. There was a remote-control television in the bedroom. Another in the sitting room. Another little one in the bathroom. There on the bathroom sink counter was a basket of exotic soaps and shampoos and other kinds of washes, plus two carefully folded wash rags and something called a shoe mitt. A round mirror that magnified things so much you could see right down inside whiskers and pores came out of the wall on a folding metal arm. A white terry-cloth robe hung on the bathroom door, with a little printed card in a pocket urging me not to steal it. "Robes may be purchased through the Concierge," it said. Whatever that was. There was nothing on the room service menu a normal person could afford. A hamburger with fries, called a Claremont Sirloin Burger with a choice of Swiss, cheddar, brie, blue or goat cheese, was $14. A Central Park Turkey Club with Ripple Chips was $19. A Pepsi, $3.50; coffee, $2.50. A piece of Park Avenue Cheesecake with something called Fresh Berry Coulis was $6.

Then I went for a walk outside on the streets around the hotel. It was just after five o'clock, and it was hot. Like the taxis, the people moved at racetrack speed. With their elbows out, their eyes straight ahead, their mouths turned down in a frozen frown. Again, I wondered what had upset everybody so. I tried to stop a man to ask directions to Radio City Music Hall, which I had seen on television and I knew was somewhere near our hotel. He raised his right hand and shook his head and said, "Nothing, buddy. Nothing. Get a job, for Chrissake." I was tempted to pick my nose, beat my chest and then holler at him that I was the lieutenant governor of Oklahoma! That would have given him a real scare.

I remembered what Curtis Mathis had told me about New York before I left. Curtis was the head of a chain of drugstores in Oklahoma. He was from Chickasha, but he had gone to college up in Connecticut or Boston or someplace and had been to New York many times.

"Being in New York is like being in heaven, a sewer, a mansion, a hovel and a movie all at once," he had said. "You can go from being scared for your life to feeling Fred Astaire–dreamy, all in one block or one minute."

I hadn't felt like Fred Astaire yet.

But he was on television back in the suite. I used the remote-control gadgets to turn on all three of the TV sets to a channel running the twenty-year-old-movie *Daddy Long Legs*. It was the singing and dancing story of a rich playboy played by Fred and a poor French waif played by Leslie Caron.

I could not imagine either Fred or Leslie ever singing a note or dancing a step in New York City.

I had left a wake-up call for seven o'clock, which was the same as six o'clock in Oklahoma because of a one-hour time difference between Eastern and Central time. Joe had said he wanted Cal and me to have breakfast with him in his suite at eight and then listen to him read his speech and read his speech and read his speech until he got it right. All day he would read it to us, if necessary. Right up until it was time to mount that podium at Madison Square Garden, if necessary.

A friendly female operator voice said: "Good morning, sir. It is seven A.M. The temperature outside is seventy-four degrees. The forecast is for sunny skies all day. So you won't need an umbrella. But dress coolly, because it will get into the low nineties before the day is over."

"Thank you," I said.

"Have a nice day," she said.

"You, too," I replied.

"Thank you."

"You're welcome."

And we hung up.

I had to choose between two soaps for my shower. There was a regular off-white bar of bath soap in a sealed plastic soap dish with a C for "Claremont" engraved in script on top. And there was a dark orange Vitabath thing wrapped in cellophane. I chose the regular. There were three shampoos to choose from. I selected Cherry Blossom Rose. It was in a plastic envelope that had to be squeezed out like those packages of mayonnaise and mustard at carry-out restaurants.

It was a good shower. The water came out of the nozzle in a strong and steady fashion. I had some trouble getting the temperature right. I had the water run out of the regular tub faucet for a while before I switched to the shower. There was a lever on the faucet that did the switching. The soap produced a fine and full lather. So did the Cherry Blossom Rose. I found the aroma left by the shampoo a little much, though. A little too much Cherry Blossom Rose.

I dried off with the softest white bath towel in the Western world. It was almost as big as one of those banners they hang over the main streets of our small towns to proclaim the coming of a Pioneer Days Parade or whatever. I put the don't-steal robe on my dry, clean, naked self and adjourned to the bedroom, where I put on a pair of jockey shorts, dark blue socks, pale blue dress shirt with button-down collar and a dark blue suit with tiny, faint light blue stripes. I had brought four ties. I selected the solid maroon. Jackie always told me it went well with my one blue eye. I would have run the shoeshine mitt over my black dress shoes, but there was no need. I had left them in a plastic bag on the doorknob outside my room before I went to bed. Somebody had taken them away while I slept, put a fabulous shine on them and then put them back.

My room was 1410. I had a huge picture window looking north over a huge park called Central Park. There were buildings on both sides and at the far end. I stood at the window for a few minutes and watched people walking and jogging through the park paths and yellow taxis springing through the park roads.

I wondered what it must be like to live in a place where you had to jog in a park right in the middle of town like that and ride around in yellow taxis with drivers making obscene gestures. Even up where I was, I could hear the noise of the brakes and the horns and the whistles and the car and truck and bus engines. I felt sorry for everyone who had to live here, and I wondered again what in the world it could possibly have to do with Fred Astaire. He was a dancer. Nobody here was dancing. They always say deep down all Americans are alike, but I was not so sure I believed that. Not so sure at all.

Joe's room was 1614. Two floors up.

It was time to go.

There were two other people already on the elevator. One was an attractive, plump woman wearing a "Marlin for Veep" button.

"Marlin?" I said. "Is he a senator?"

"She's a she," said the woman. "She works in the district catalogue office in St. Louis."

"So it isn't for veep of the United States?"

She laughed. "No, no. The Sears employee credit union board. We're having our annual meeting. I'm from Oil City, Pennsylvania. I love coming here. Don't you? Where are you from?"

"Oklahoma."

"Gloria Grahame was always my favorite."

Gloria Grahame played the part of Ado Annie in the movie version of the musical *Oklahoma!* Gordon MacRae played Curly, Shirley Jones was Laurie, Rod Steiger was Jud Fry, and Gene Nelson was Will. We once had a defected Soviet KGB man living in Oklahoma who knew all of the words to all of the songs in *Oklahoma!* His mother had been a big fan of Broadway musicals and she had taught the songs to him on the sly when he was growing up. That was why he had chosen Oklahoma to live in after he had come over to our side. But that is another whole story.

The elevator stopped at 15. And the woman got off.

The other passenger was an older man in a tuxedo who was reading a paperback book entitled *Great Stories from the Dead*."

"Here for the convention?" I asked.

"What convention?" he replied.

"The Democrats."

"I'm a bartender downstairs."

The elevator arrived at 16. I got off and walked down a long hall and then took a left to Joe's room.

"How about this for living?" Joe said the second I walked in. "How about this for the First Man of Oklahoma, the Keynoter of the Democratic Party? How about it, Mack?"

"Great, Joe. Great and only fitting," I said after looking around. I decided not to tell him my room was as big as his. It would have upset him, and why upset him on this most, most important day of his life?

Cal was already there. He was in his regular jeans-shirt-boots getup. Joe was wearing pajamas and robe and slippers. The robe was another of the hotel's white terry-cloth ones, like mine. His pajamas were dark-brown-and-yellow-striped. Like what prison inmates in a comic strip might wear. His slippers were tan and were made out of some kind of thin plastic or cardboard. I wondered if the hotel had provided them, and if so, where were mine?

And I was struck by the fact that in the seven years Joe and I had served side by side as First Man and Second Man of Oklahoma, this was the first time I had seen him in pajamas, robe and slippers.

He said:

"Take that coat and tie off, Mack. We have work to do for Oklahoma. For the Democratic Party. For America. Do you know how many people will be watching me tonight? Do you, Mack? Do you?"

"No, Joe, I don't."

"Look at this."

He handed me a copy of a newspaper that had been folded over and down a couple of times to display just a few magic words of a very long story.

Those magic words said:

> All three networks plan to go back and forth from the podium activities to interviews on the floor and outside the convention hall itself. But they said they would definitely stay on the podium for the keynote address, which is to be given by Governor Joe Hayman of Oklahoma, a moderate conservative known for his rhetorical flourishes. He is also believed to be on Senator Griffin's short list of possibilities for vice-president.
>
> Network programmers estimate their combined

prime-time audiences tonight will number more than 80 million.

"Wow," I said.

"Wow is right. The Short List. How short? Has there ever in history been a time when eighty million people all at one time saw and heard an Oklahoman?"

"Sure," Cal said. "Will Rogers."

"That was on the radio. I mean heard and seen. I mean a politician," Joe said.

"Will Rogers thought politicians were jokes," Cal said.

"It's good you're rich and have a DC-9, or I'd drop you like a chewed-on chicken bone, Cal Blackwell."

"I want to be an ambassador, remember," Cal said.

"To where?" Joe asked.

"Anywhere."

"I'll get you a price list after I'm vice-president."

Joe and Cal laughed, and I removed my coat and tie. Joe motioned Cal and me to take chairs before a desk he had moved in front of his picture window. He stepped behind the desk and turned his back on Central Park to face us. The desk was his podium. We were his audience.

He opened a manila folder to his speech. He looked out to us. He smiled. Cal and I applauded. Joe acknowledged it.

"Mr. Chairman. Mr. Chairman. It is with a profound sense of history, humility and honor that I keynote this convention of the party of all the people of this great United States of America. The Democratic Party, which is *the* party of all of the United States of America ..."

And off he went, for twenty-seven minutes. He tried to pause when he thought there might be applause and cheers. He tried to smile when he thought there might be laughter.

He tried to put in rhetorical flourishes where he thought there ought to be rhetorical flourishes.

We critiqued him.

"Relax, Joe," Cal said. "You're tight. How many speeches have you made in your life?"

"Shut up, Cal," Joe said. "Don't try to tell me making the Keynote Address at the Democratic National Convention in New York City at Madison Square Garden before ten thousand people with another eighty million watching on television is just like talking to the Kingfisher Kiwanis. Don't say it, Cal. Because if you say it, that will finally prove to me what everybody else in Oklahoma has been trying to tell me for years. And that is that you are a certified lunatic who not only thinks it's normal to have blue 1949 Packards parked in circles in the middle of a pasture..."

"It's 1948, Joe," Cal said. "They're 1948 Packards, not '49s. They changed the sweep of the fenders in '49."

Joe looked to me for help. For anything.

"Why don't we try it again, Joe," I said.

So he went through it again.

He seemed even tenser. His voice was rising in pitch. His gestures got way out of hand. A couple of times he threw his right arm and fist into the air with such gusto I thought he might throw something out of joint.

"It's getting worse, Joe," Cal said. "Why don't you take a swallow or two of bourbon or something?"

"Shut up, Cal."

We were saved for the moment by a knock on the door. It was a room service crew with breakfast. Joe had ordered it before I arrived.

Two young dark-skinned men in white coats and black pants and bow ties wheeled a table into the room. There were rollers on the legs, so the table moved easily and quietly over the carpet, which was thick and solid purple. The one in my room was a light burgundy—almost pink. There was a small round dining table already in the room, so all the two young men did was transfer plates, silverware, a small bunch of roses in a vase and all the rest to it. The food was a huge platter of gooey, undercooked scrambled eggs and bacon, and a basket of Danish, croissants and three or four kinds of muffins including one that Cal said was carrot-flavored. Plus a pitcher of orange juice sitting in a bowl of crushed ice, two silver pots of coffee, several jars of jams and preserves, and a dish of pats of butter that were as hard as cast iron. Until they had chance to melt a bit.

"I knew you hated all eggs but scrambled," Joe said to me. "I knew you hated everything but bacon and corn muffins," he said to Cal. "So here we are."

Cal signed the check, which was for $47.50 plus a twenty-percent tip. The two young men left and we sat down to eat.

"Has anyone ever thrown up while making a keynote speech?" Cal said after I had taken my first bite of egg. "I mean, right there at the microphone while speaking the words that were going out over the airwaves to all Americans?" I do not have the strongest stomach in the world; the eggs were too watery for my taste and I had to hold my breath.

"Shut up, Cal," Joe said.

"I have never ever seen you this screwed up and around," said Cal. "You're going to explode."

"I have never, ever keynoted a national convention of the Democratic Party before eighty million people."

"I think you should take something to calm down. You're going to blow a gasket. . . . "

"No drugs. No drugs."

"All right, no drugs. How about some Valium?"

"That's a drug. That's a drug."

"Doctors prescribe them in Tulsa like they're peanuts."

"This is not Tulsa, thank God, and I don't like peanuts. Shut up, Cal."

The phone rang. I started to get up to answer it. Joe waved me back down. "Jill's in the bedroom. She'll get it. Nobody but Griffin and Jesus Christ get through to me this day."

The door to a bedroom opened. Jill Hayman, fully dressed and holding a magazine, stuck her head out. "It's for you, Cal."

"No calls, Jill. No calls..."

"Who is it from?" Cal asked.

"He said to tell you it was Mercer about the Packard in Yuma."

Cal was up and moving toward the phone on the desk. "I'll take it. Thanks, Jill." She ducked back into the bedroom.

"Look here!" boomed Joe. "We are here to keynote the national convention of the Democratic Party of the United States of America! Not to make deals for old cars!"

Cal smiled, winked at me and picked up the phone. Joe and I had no choice but to listen to his every word.

"Hey, Mercer, this is Blackwell. What have you got?" He listened. "It's a deal. I'll wire the money this afternoon.... Anything else?" He listened again. "No, not interested. Only my blue '48 Packards..."

Cal looked around directly at me and then said into the phone, "Wait a minute. I may have somebody who would be interested."

He put his right hand over the phone's mouthpiece and said: "Mack, listen to this. Mercer's run onto a guy with five identical red 1957 Ford Fairlane four-doors. He'll part with

77

all five for ten grand, FOB some little town called Camden over in Arkansas. They'd be quite a starter on a very special collection. What do you say?"

"No, really, Cal. I can't afford . . ."

"Cal! God damn it!" Joe screamed. "Hang up that phone!"

"I'll take them," Cal said into the receiver. "Money and instructions will be on the way soon."

He rejoined us at the breakfast table. Joe's face, always mostly white, was now mostly pink.

"Cal, you are an idiot. I mean you are an idiot. Here you are with . . ."

"I've got something for you, Joe." Cal reached into his shirt pocket and pulled out a small silver container about an inch square that looked like it was for stick matches. He pushed its tiny drawer open and took out a tiny round yellow pill.

"Take it, Joe. Take it before you explode into a million tiny pieces."

"I am antidrug. You know that. My picture is on billboards from Guymon to Vinita telling the young people of Oklahoma not to get high on drugs or drink."

Cal was holding the pill up in front of himself between the thumb and forefinger of his right hand. "Taking one little Valium does not make you a drug addict, Joe. For God's sake and your own sake."

"Where did you get those pills, anyhow?"

"I bought 'em from a guy in Oklahoma City."

"What guy?"

"He's a former cop who works security at the stockyards. Why?"

"He's a drug dealer, Cal. A drug dealer. That's why. You bought them from a drug dealer. Cal! God damn it, Cal!" Joe put his hands to his ears so he couldn't hear anymore.

"Why not go through the speech again?" I said.

"Right. The speech. Let me go through the speech again. Right."

I exchanged very troubled glances with Cal, as Joe resumed his speaking position with his back to Central Park.

Joe kept us there as his captive audience for the rest of the day. He recited his speech another sixteen times. Really, sixteen. I kept count. Six of them were between the end of breakfast and the beginning of lunch. We were allowed to order our own room service lunch. I had a fourteen-dollar Palm Beach Tuna Fish Sandwich on wheat bread. It came with a handful of rippled potato chips, a huge dill pickle and a scoop of cole slaw. I also had a Pepsi again, because they didn't have Grapette or Dr Pepper. I knew a kid back in Kansas who poured salted peanuts down the Pepsi bottle before he drank from it, and I wondered what he would think if he saw me now. Cal drank two Buds and ate a Claremont Sirloin Burger with lettuce, tomato and mayonnaise. Joe got a nine-ounce rib-eye steak with french fries and salad, but he never touched any of it.

After lunch came another quick five run-throughs of the speech. Then, in midafternoon, Joe announced a break so he could lie down for a while. He told Cal and me not to leave the room, just in case he couldn't sleep and he needed us. So Cal got on the phone and I stretched out on one of the three couches in the sitting room. Joe was gone for less than fifteen minutes.

"Okay, men, let's go at it again," he said when he was ready. He was still in his pajamas, robe and slippers. His face was now a deep pink.

"I think we should turn on the television and watch a

movie or something," Cal said to Joe. "You have got that speech down cold. You could practice it another hundred times and it would not get any better. It's perfect. Cool it before you lose it."

I agreed with Cal. I said, "That's right, Joe. You have got it made...."

Joe walked behind the desk and with his back to Central Park began again.

"Mr. Chairman. Mr. Chairman. It is with a profound sense of history, humility and honor that I keynote this convention of the party of all of the people of this great United States of America. The Democratic Party, which is *the* party of the United States of America..."

And again and again another five times straight.

I found that my lips were now moving with his when he talked. So were Cal's. We now knew it as well as Joe did.

"Mr. Chairman. Mr. Chairman. It is with a profound sense of history, humility and honor..."

Joe finally let Cal and me go just before six o'clock, with instructions to be back in his room at eight for the ride to Madison Square Garden.

His parting words to me were: "I decided to wear a blue suit, Mack. A blue suit. Brown simply will not work at the national level. Not here at the national level. Blue it is. I have it, and you and Cal will be among the first to see me in it. Jill, of course, will be the very first. The very first. God, how I wished they would let her sing 'God Bless America' tonight. I need that tonight. I really do need it, Mack."

5
. . .
TWENTY-NINE MINUTES

I had watched Joe come through in all kinds of difficult situations. I had seen him stand up in front of hostile farmers, irate teachers, pompous bankers, posturing lawyers, sanctimonious preachers and other screaming ninnies of our beloved Oklahoma political process, and always prevail, always leave them wondering what in the world it was that they were upset with Buffalo Joe Hayman about in the first place. I had watched him speak to multitudes in rainshowers, in 105-degree heat, in places where the PA had been stolen, where there were more Republicans than Democrats, more Catholics than Baptists and Holy Roads, more illiterates than not. I was there that day in Stillwater when a group of hippie freak liberals from out of state tried—much, much in vain—to shout him down when he talked about sending people to the electric chair for selling marijuana to minors. I was also in the Methodist church in Ardmore when he delivered the funeral eulogy for Sally Lee Hendricks, the widow of an old political friend, who had gone off to California as a teenager to be a movie star and come back thirty years later with her only claim being that she had been the stand-in for Ingrid Bergman in *Casablanca*. Her sister, who was older and crazy, had started screaming while Joe was eulogizing Sally. She had run up to the pulpit yelling, "You are the devil! You are the devil! You killed my Sally!" She took a couple of swings at Joe. He threw his big arms around her and held her in a bear hug while she cried and cried there in front of everybody. Then he turned back to the congregation and finished his eulogy with her there in his arms.

He always conquered. He always pulled it off. And I was sure he would do so again.

Although I had to admit to myself that Joe was right that keynoting a Democratic National Convention at Madison Square Garden on television before eighty million people was different from anything he had ever done before.

"Mr. Chairman. It is with a profound sense of history, humility and honor that I keynote..."

I could not get those words out of my head. Those and all the rest. I could hear Joe's voice:

"Mr. Chairman. It is with a profound sense of history, humility and honor that I keynote this convention of..."

I went back to my room hearing it. I undressed down to my underwear hearing it. I carefully hung up my good blue dress shirt hearing it. I climbed into bed hearing it.

I closed my eyes hearing it.

"Mr. Chairman. It is with a profound sense of history, humility and honor that I keynote this convention..."

I picked up the phone, dialed 8 and then Jackie's office back in Oklahoma City. For some strange reason, she and I never had done well on the telephone. A little electric tension got on the line, especially when it was long-distance, the second we started talking. Innocent remarks got taken wrong, slights got imagined, levels of interest got read wrongly, and so on. One time she was away at a board of governors meeting of the Southwest Grocers Association in Fort Worth. I caught her in her room at the Hotel Worthington just as she was about to go to Cattlemen's restaurant for dinner with her fellow governors. I said hi; she barely said it back. She wondered what was eating me. I said, Nothing, why? Well, that tone, she said. I said, Just now when I said hi? That's right, she said. You sounded like you were about to chew my head off. . . . We went on like that for ten minutes or so, until she ended it by screaming that she was already late for the dinner, and slamming the receiver down.

This time I did the slamming.

The tension was right there again the second I said, Hi from New York City the Largest City in the World, and she said, Hi from Oklahoma City the Best City in *My* World. She tried to tell me about developments in the Hammerschmidt of Trailways merger idea, and I tried to tell her about Joe and his speech.

After I gave her a detailed report on Joe's maniacal obsession with saying that speech over and over, her only comment was:

"Yes, Mack. But that's not surprising. Joe's always been a fool and always will be. You should be the governor of Oklahoma and he should be the lieutenant governor—or your chauffeur. Hammerschmidt did have a favor to ask you if I happened to talk to you."

"Well, you happen to be talking to me."

"I am indeed. He wondered if you might be able to persuade Joe to come out in his keynote speech in favor of privatizing the postal service. Maybe even mention that it could be done in conjunction with private companies in the parcel delivery, drive-thru grocery and intercity bus businesses. He wouldn't have to mention Trailways and us by name. Hammerschmidt thinks the competition would not have time to move before we did, because we are already so far ahead. He thinks the risk is worth it for that kind of national visibility before all of those politicians and the millions of other Americans watching on the television...."

It was about then that I said I had to run to an appointment or something, and slammed the receiver down.

And I suddenly so much wanted one of Cal's Valiums. I had never, ever used one or anything else like it, but I knew what it might be able to do for me.

I got up and went to the window. Central Park was still there. So were the yellow taxis and the walkers and the joggers, presumably screaming at each other and exchanging their favorite obscene gestures.

Back in bed, I closed my eyes again. I tried to think of Fred Astaire and Leslie Caron dancing across the street in that Central Park.

"Mr. Chairman. It is with a profound sense of history, humility and honor..."

I dialed Cal's room.

"Cal, this is Mack. Can I have one of those Valium things?" I said in a whisper. Like I was contracting a murder. "I can't rest for hearing that speech in my brain like a wailing siren...."

"I'll be right down," he said. And he was.

I had trouble looking him in the eye. But I took the pill and we went to the bathroom, where I swallowed it with a glass of water. He said his bathroom was exactly like mine.

And he said he had chosen to use the Cherry Blossom Rose shampoo rather than Lemon Mist or Raspberry Tart Spray. What about me? I confirmed that Cherry Blossom Rose was my choice, too. The Valium had a metallic taste. Like tinfoil.

"This will not make you a drug addict, Mack, I promise," said Cal. "All it will do is get you through the ordeal of Joe's speech. My God, have you ever seen anything like it? He needs a hobby. Maybe playing basketball at lunch or something."

"If I had to guess, I would say Joe has never set two feet on a basketball court," I said. I was waiting to be knocked out from the Valium. Nothing yet.

"Wrong. He played in college. A guard. Good dribbling and ball handling."

"I think I'm going to lie down now. Thanks for . . . well, your help. Do I owe you anything?"

He laughed. "Mack, please. And don't worry. You have done nothing wrong. It's like borrowing a squirt of somebody's toothpaste."

I had never borrowed a squirt of toothpaste from anybody other than Jackie. He left and I got back on the bed.

Joe's voice and words were there again. "Mr. Chairman. It is with a profound sense of history . . ."

But after a while it got fainter. I saw Fred and Leslie, the couple on the bed at the Enid Best Western, Sandra Faye Parsons, David E. George, alias John Wilkes Booth, tied to a chair, and finally I dozed off.

We left the Claremont in the gray limousine a few minutes after eight o'clock. All six of us had ridden in the back coming in from the airport, but this time I got up front with the driver so Joe could be alone with Jill, their sons and Cal.

There were jumpseats that came folding down to face the backseat.

Cal was in the jumpseat on the right, behind me. We had gone less than a block when he opened the window between the front and the back and said: "Ask the driver what happened to the little TV. It's gone. Joe wants to see if they're talking about him yet."

I passed the question on to the driver.

"Somebody stole it. I was parked over on the East Side and went into a place for a cup of coffee, and somebody stole it. Can you imagine? Right in broad daylight. Broke in and took it."

I had barely noticed him earlier. He was a swarthy man in his fifties. He was dressed in a black suit with a matching billed cap like a bus driver's, only without the badge and metal visor stripe.

I passed his answer on to Cal, who then closed the window.

"There're a lot of sick and mean people out there," said the driver. "Maybe everybody out there is a little sick and mean. Look at 'em."

We were headed down a wide one-way street that was full of people and neon advertising for movies and cameras.

"Times Square?" I asked.

"Times Square," he said. "Not a well person anywhere within ten blocks of this place. Not within ten blocks of this place." I was tempted to tell him that the man in back also tended to repeat himself a lot.

"You people in politics?" he asked.

"Yes, sir," I replied.

"People in politics always say they're going to do something about the sickness, but they never do. They never do. They can't. You want to know why?"

"Yes, sir."

"Because they're as sick as the rest of us. Sicker. Some of them way sicker. Everybody's sick. Look at that."

I looked at a young couple kissing madly and rubbing up against each other on a street corner.

"What are you people in politics doing about that kind of thing? Nothing, is what you are doing. I know why. You want to know why?"

"Yes, sir."

"Because you politicians don't think that's sick. Neither do I. None of us do. But it is. Nothing that is sick seems sick anymore because we're used to it. But it's still sick. You people in politics have gotten used to too much. You're as sick as the rest of us now."

"Yes, sir," I said.

I glanced back through the window at Buffalo Joe Hayman, governor of Oklahoma and keynote speaker of the Democratic National Convention. He looked great in his new dark blue suit. His lips were moving. There was no sound, but I could read along. "Mr. Chairman. It is with a profound sense of history, humility and honor that I keynote this convention of the party of all the people of this great United States of America. The Democratic Party, which is *the* party of all of the United States of America . . ."

We had a special vehicle permit in the windshield of the car. Policemen saw it, then removed some wooden barricades and waved us right up to an entrance marked ADMISSION BLUE CREDENTIALS ONLY.

Several people appeared and started opening the limo doors.

"Welcome, Governor," somebody said to Joe. "Welcome, Governor. Ready for your big night?"

Joe smiled and nodded. He looked like he might throw up.

We followed a couple of young men in dark suits with plastic earpiece things in their ears and yellow-and-green buttons in their lapels down and around gray concrete corridors and up and down flights of gray concrete stairs. Occasionally I heard the noise of people talking and yelling coming from somewhere. And music from a band. We were close to the convention floor.

"Mr. Chairman. It is with a profound sense of history, humility and honor that I keynote this convention . . ."

Finally, we came to a door marked KEYNOTE SPEAKER. The two young men opened it and ushered us inside. It was a room the size of the average suburban Oklahoma City family room. There were ten of those canvas-and-wooden chairs movie directors supposedly sit in while yelling at movie stars. There had been one in a corner of that room at the Enid Best Western, if I remembered correctly. These were carefully arranged in two sets of five around two low-slung black plastic coffee tables. A large television set was on a table against one wall. A coffee machine and a stack of white Styrofoam cups were on a small table against another wall.

The sound was way down on the television. But I could see Speaker Andrews, chairman of the convention, pounding the gavel. There were shots of people milling around and about. Then John Chancellor and David Brinkley came on the screen. They said a few words to each other. A Chrysler commercial was next.

Then a young blonde woman in her late teens or early twenties appeared in the room. She had several passes encrusted in plastic hanging by a small chain around her neck.

"Governor Hayman?" she said to the room.

We all pointed to Joe.

She walked over to him. She was shaking like she was doing an oral book report on a book she hadn't quite finished reading. "Sir, I am the page assigned to take you from here to the waiting area right behind the podium. I will do so when I am instructed to by the chairman. It should only be a few minutes now."

Joe nodded. His coloring was now a grapefruit pink. His eyes were expressionless. I could tell he was now at full-bore concentration on those words: "Mr. Chairman. It is with a profound sense of history, humility and honor . . ."

The young woman, her face also pink with anxiety now, left the room.

"Well, Joe, only a few more beats of the heart and there you'll be," Cal said.

Jill Hayman had not said a word since we arrived. The color of her hair had changed to a deep pitch-black since I'd last seen her that afternoon. She was wearing a fully unfurled pink dress that resembled a stage curtain in its size and arrangement across and around her body. She reached over and grabbed Joe's left hand. It was a gesture of transfusion, it seemed to me. Here, take a little strength from me. Here, dear. Right from me to you, like a tube carrying Phillips 66 Super Unleaded, here it comes, Joe. Hold on now. Here it comes. You are going to be just fine. God Bless America from me to you, Joe dear.

The two sons turned up the sound on the television.

Brinkley and Chancellor were back. "Keynote speeches have been known to make political careers, have they not, David?" Chancellor said.

"That's right. Frank Church in 1960. Even back to Alben

Barkley in 1948. Truman supposedly chose him for the ticket because he made such a great speech. . . ."

I hopped up and turned down the sound again.

Speaker Andrews was pounding the gavel again.

The door to our room opened again.

It was the attractive young blonde page again.

She walked up to Joe. Her feet came together like she had been called to attention by some army sergeant. In a screech she said: "Governor Hayman. The chairman of this convention, the speaker of the house, Mark T. Andrews of Georgia, wishes to inform you that this convention of the Democratic Party awaits the pleasure of your Keynote Address. If you will come with me, sir?"

The next few minutes are in my memory like a never-ending TV replay.

With his left hand, Joe picked up the folder that had his speech in it. He stood. He took one step. Then another. His face went Oklahoma-clay red. Suddenly. Like somebody had turned on a switch. Then it locked in a horrified stare. He grabbed the left side of his head. His eyes closed.

And he fell backward. Stiff. Like a tree falling. His head hit the concrete floor. Whack!

The young page screamed and ran out yelling, "Doctor! Doctor! Where is a doctor?"

Cal, Jill and I went to Joe.

Jill yelled: "Joe! No, Joe! What's wrong? Joe!"

"He just fainted," Cal said, trying to put an arm around her shoulders.

"Right. Nerves," I said. I took my dark blue suitcoat off and folded it twice and stuck it under his head. It gave me a chance to check if he was still breathing. He was. Normally, almost, it seemed.

Then a man in a white coat raced in.

"One side, please. I am a doctor."

We all moved so he could get in. He had a small black leather bag. Right behind him came four men with a portable stretcher. Clearly, a full medical team was in attendance for the convention.

Thank God.

The doctor was a man in his forties. He had the hands of a magician. In a matter of seconds, he had felt Joe's pulse, listened to his heart with a stethoscope and stuck something under his nose.

Joe opened his eyes. The color of his face was almost back to its normal linen-white.

"How do you feel?" the doctor asked.

Joe moved his lips, but there was no sound. He tried again. Tears came to his eyes.

"He's had a mild stroke, most likely," said the doctor. "Temporary problem, probably. Has he been under any tension?"

Has he been under any tension?

"Stand aside for the speaker," some loud male voice thundered.

The next second I looked up to the face of Mark T. Andrews of Georgia, speaker of the U.S. House of Representatives and chairman of the Democratic National Convention.

"Governor Hayman, are you all right?" he asked.

"He's had a bad fall, apparently," said the doctor. "Some temporary problems. He cannot respond to your question."

"Sorry, Governor," said the speaker. "Sorry about the speech. I'm sure it would have been a great one to hear. Please, on behalf of all of us here at this convention and of all Democrats and other Americans everywhere, please accept our best wishes for a speedy recovery."

Joe's face was now in an excited state. He was still grasping the speech folder in his left hand. He thrust it toward me.

Then he motioned for something to write with. The doctor handed him a white ballpoint pen, one of those with a tiny clicker on top for lowering the point. It had "Ritz-Carlton Hotel" inscribed on it, and I wondered where and how he had gotten it.

Joe clicked it and scribbled across the folder: "Mack give speech."

Speaker Andrews read the words and then said to me, "You are Mack?"

"Yes, sir."

"Who exactly are you, Mack?"

"I am the lieutenant governor of Oklahoma, sir."

Andrews, clearly faced with a monumental decision, looked up and around and down in hopes of finding a pair of familiar eyes that could help him make it. There weren't any. It was up to him.

"Can you do it?" he finally said to me.

"He knows it cold," said Cal.

"It's on the TelePrompTer," said the blonde page.

"I really would rather not," I said.

Joe was moving his head back and forth. His eyes had a look of fury in them. His face was turning red again.

So, I said, "Yes, I would rather not. But I must say it would be with a profound sense of history, humility and honor that I would keynote this convention of the party of all the people of this great United States of America. The Democratic Party, which is *the* party of all of the United States of America."

"Come with me, Mack," said the speaker of the House.

I took the speech folder from Joe, shook his right hand, stood up and followed the speaker out to deliver the Keynote Address to the Democratic National Convention at Madison

Square Garden in New York City before a national television audience of eighty million people.

All I heard as I walked out the door was Cal. "You're the best, Mack," he said. "You're an Oklahoma hero."

I was a good ten yards down the hall when I heard Cal yelling after me to wait. I turned around. He had my suitcoat.

"You're going to need this," he said, handing it to me.

"Thanks, Cal."

"You're a hero, Mack."

He slapped me on the shoulder.

And I walked on, thinking only:

"Mr. Chairman. It is with a profound sense of history, humility and honor ..."

Speaker Andrews asked me to stand at the bottom of the stairs leading up to the podium. He went on up by himself. The young blonde page stood by my side staring at me like she was afraid all Oklahomans were afflicted with the same disease that Joe had and that maybe I might keel over, too. But she did manage to tell me that news about a problem with the keynote speaker had already spread to the floor and upstairs to Chancellor and Brinkley and the other TV people in their booths and thus to all of America.

I wondered about what the people back in Oklahoma must be thinking. I wondered what they had been told by Chancellor and Brinkley and the others.

I wondered what they were going to think when they saw their one-eyed lieutenant governor march to the podium.

Andrews had to hit his gavel only three times. Suddenly the place was silent like a church. The page was right. The convention knew something was up.

The speaker, a man who liked his drama, said: "Please,

ladies and gentlemen of this convention, Democrats everywhere, Americans everywhere who are watching on television . . . please bow your heads in a silent prayer for our
beloved friend and public servant Governor Joe Hayman of
Oklahoma."

I could hear a huge gasp.

There was silence for a solid minute. All the way to Oklahoma, I was sure.

Then Andrews said: "Our keynote speaker has been taken
ill." I couldn't see him, but Andrews must have looked over
at our Oklahoma delegation. "But doctors say it is an illness
from which he is most likely to recover fully."

Somebody from the Oklahoma delegation cheered. Then
a few others and some more did. And finally it sounded to
me like everybody in Madison Square Garden was cheering
or clapping. It meant the rumor that had spread through the
convention must have been that he was dead. Joe Hayman,
the keynote speaker, was dead. Now he wasn't.

Andrews waited a few seconds for the crowd to settle down
before he told the ladies and gentlemen of the convention,
Democrats everywhere, Americans everywhere that Governor
Hayman's keynote speech would be delivered at the governor's own request by the lieutenant governor of Oklahoma.

The young blonde page looked at me and then motioned
with her head for me to go up the stairs. She was much more
afraid than I was. Maybe she now thought what Joe had was
contagious. And all Oklahomans were carriers.

My confidence wavered a bit as my left foot hit the last
step. My leg shook a bit. I thought for a second it might give
way. And there I'd go, falling flat on my face. Maybe what
Joe had really *was* contagious!

Much of the crowd was on its feet, cheering and clapping.
Trying to make me feel good, urging me on.

I wondered how many of them had ever seen a one-eyed lieutenant governor before.

"Mr. Chairman. It is with profound Oklahoma pride, humility and honor . . ."

I walked to the podium. Speaker Andrews shook my hand with both of his, like Joe did, like Jed Berryhill the movie producer did, like even Sandra Faye Parsons did.

There were a small fluorescent reading light and two microphones sticking up at me. I put the speech folder down and opened it. I looked out, and there were the words of the speech staring back at me from three TelePrompTers. "Mr. Chairman. It is with a profound sense of history, humility and honor . . ." They were projected up in front of me and there on the left and the right. I had never read a thing off a TelePrompTer before. The whole idea of it annoyed me. I always figured that if you didn't know what you wanted to say well enough to speak it from memory, then at least be honest enough not to try to fake it like you did. Just go ahead and read it like real people do. I think Lyndon Johnson was the first president to use one in public speeches, and that started it. The whole idea of public officials using them for speeches was an insult, and stupid. I don't know why the American people let them get away with such nonsense. People in audiences should just start shouting at them: "Read it! Just read it off the paper!"

I certainly did not need a TelePrompTer. I had the words of the speech so dug into my brain there was no way I could ever forget them.

I looked beyond the TelePrompTer words to the faces of thousands of Democrats in red-white-and-blue hats with their state standards and signs. There was real silence. I never knew that many people could be so quiet anywhere, especially at a political convention.

I had to say something first about the extraordinary special situation that had brought me to this position as keynote speaker of the Democratic National Convention at Madison Square Garden before them and a television audience estimated to number at least eighty million.

So I did some minor extemporaneous editing.

"It is with a profound sense of Oklahoma pride, humility and honor that I stand before you now in place of our great governor, a man who has been felled by the rock of disease. But only temporarily. There is no disease wicked and worse and Republican enough to do anything permanent to Joseph Mark Hayman of Buffalo, Oklahoma."

You would have thought I had cracked the funniest joke of the century. They laughed and hooted and whistled and stomped their feet. It sounded like thunder was erupting from under the floor. And I suddenly had the exhilarating feeling that most of the eighty million watching on television were doing the same thing at their homes or wherever they were watching.

I had always had a good voice. Deep, like my dad's and radio announcers'. And I had through the years in politics learned some of the basic things about gesturing and smiling and raising and lowering the volume and the pitch and the tone. In other words, I was not that ill at ease over making speeches. I was a good speaker. But the thunder and knowing that all of those people were listening in this extraordinary special situation suddenly gave me an extraordinary special power of speech I did not know existed in me or anyone else.

Joe's words—Cow Cowell's words—flowed out of my mouth like they were part of a majestic golden stream to Glory.

I spoke of America the Beautiful, Russia the Wicked, China

the Evil. I rolled through lists of Democratic accomplishments and Republican obstructions from the beginning of history. I quoted John Fitzgerald Kennedy and Franklin Delano Roosevelt and Harry S. Truman. I slammed weakness and timidity and praised action and boldness. I demanded jail for the thugs and jobs for the poor.

I spoke in rolls and thunders and whispers. I cited Genesis and Ecclesiastes, Ernest Hemingway, a writer who killed himself, and Will Rogers, who died in a plane crash with Wiley Post, another Oklahoman. I looked to the heavens, I scowled, I smiled, I pointed, I flung my fists, I pounded, I wiped my forehead with a handkerchief.

I was interrupted several times—twenty-two, to be absolutely accurate—with applause and foot stomping.

There was a slight echo in the hall, and a few times I paused to listen to my own sounds sail up and around that Madison Square Garden and out through the windows and doors and cracks to all of America. It reminded me of the first big speech I ever gave. It was on the courthouse lawn in Adabel at the ceremony where Jackie received Pepper's Congressional Medal of Honor and Purple Heart from a Marine officer. I wasn't anything then but Pepper and Jackie's very sad best friend. My voice floated gently like smoke through the trees and over the dry goods and furniture and Rexall stores and the newspaper office on the square. I thought at the time it probably didn't even stop at the city limits and probably kept floating all the way to Utoka, forty-five miles away.

Now here I was, believe it or not, on this stage at Madison Square Garden. Here I was, living the most glorious twenty-nine minutes in the sun any American of any kind could ever even dream of living.

Here I was, just the one-eyed lieutenant governor of Oklahoma.

And I got carried away. It happened at the very end, while I was talking about a search for honesty and integrity in government, a search for answers to the serious questions of education and housing and the other problems of our time and place. Suddenly, spontaneously, I said: "And we in Oklahoma have our own special search under way for something very special to our history, to our heritage. It is for the remains of a person. A person who died in Enid, Oklahoma, in January 1903. He died of his own hand. He died with the story of a presidential assassination on his lips. His name was David E. George, but he said to some that he was in fact John Wilkes Booth and that another man had died and been buried in his place. Was he telling the truth? Was he the real John Wilkes Booth? We do not know, because the body of David E. George, perfectly preserved by an Enid mortician as were mummies in olden times, has disappeared. But we know deep down in our Oklahoma souls that it is still out there somewhere. If someone—anyone in hearing distance of my voice—knows where that body is, please let us know. Please contact the Oklahoma Historical Society. Please help us return a little bit of us to its proper home. Someone out there has in their home, their basement, their attic, their office a mummy that rightfully belongs in Enid, Oklahoma. Would you please help us find that person and help us return it to Enid? Please?"

"Yes!" someone yelled back. "Hey, hey, hey!" screamed somebody else. "Hey, hey, yes, yes! Hey, hey, yes, yes!" A chant got started. "Find the mummy, find the mummy! Hey, hey, yes, yes! Find the mummy, find the mummy! Hey, hey, yes, yes!"

It went on for a good three or four minutes. I held up both hands to end it. And I said: "Thank you, my fellow Democrats, my fellow Americans, for your attention. Pray, oh, please pray, for the safe recovery of our beloved governor. And let's work together to make sure that on election day we have a country that is Democratic with a capital D, from every courthouse in the land to the one and only White House of the land. Thank you very much."

I swear to you that right there before my very eye and ears, Madison Square Garden erupted into an uproar seldom seen anywhere but at football games.

Those wonderful Democrats from all fifty states went on for more than fifteen minutes with their marching and shouting and clapping and whistling. Speaker Andrews stayed up there with me and we waved to the crowd together. First to one side of the hall, then to the other. Then to those in the back. To those up in the stands. Then reversing the order. I always made an especially long wave when we came to the Oklahoma delegation, which had a position fairly close up on the right.

I was sure Jackie and the kids were watching. I hadn't had time to call and tell them I was doing this, but they would have tuned in to see and hear Joe anyhow. I hoped that Dad and my sister and her family in Kansas were seeing me— and it. I wondered if Joe was still alive and if he had watched me give his speech and was now watching me receive his applause, cheers and sun. I would go directly and immediately to the hospital to see him afterward.

I wondered if the people of Oklahoma were as happy about what I had done as these people in Madison Square Garden were.

Finally Speaker Andrews said in my left ear: "I think you can withdraw now."

I nodded and waved several more times as I walked to the steps and back down to the blonde page.

She was smiling and beside herself.

"David Brinkley just nominated you for vice-president," she shrieked. "David Brinkley said you'd be great for the Short List. Somebody who heard him say it on television just told me. David Brinkley! The funny one."

There was nobody else around except two of those young men in dark suits with earpieces. It was a security area and nobody else was allowed. The page turned me over to them. I told them what I wanted to do, they spoke into walkie-talkies, and I followed them back through the corridors and up and down the stairways to the long gray limousine.

It was there that Cliff Bearden came into my life. One of the security men asked if I wanted to talk to a man with credentials who was a professor of some kind. Sure, I said. They brought over a man in his mid-thirties who must have thought it was December rather than July in New York, because he was dressed in pleated tan corduroy pants and a brown-green-and-black plaid wool sport coat. His shoes were buckskin, and his face was round, fresh and so excited.

"I am director of the Center for the Study of the Speech in American Political Life at Duluth Community College in Minnesota," he said. "We have just inaugurated a new research project on the keynote speech at political conventions. Can I first tell you that was one of the great ones of all time? Can I second say congratulations. Can I third please ask if I could come to Oklahoma and interview you for oral-history purposes on what you did and how you did it and what you think about it? I want detail. I want everything. We are simple scholars, we will make our material available to researchers and historians and the ages. Will you help us preserve you for history? I can already tell you no one has ever advertised for a mummy in a keynote speech. I know that already. You made history tonight. You really did. Will you cooperate?"

I told him sure, and that I could be reached next week and thereafter and probably forevermore at the Lieutenant Governor's Office in Oklahoma City.

Bearden winked at me with his whole head as well as his left eye. And he said: "Maybe not, if Brinkley's right, and I think he is. Maybe not. I'd like to say that lastly."

He was escorted away and I stepped out into an open area. And like an avalanche of madmen they came at me. Reporters with TV cameras and microphones, reporters with only notebooks and pens. "Is the governor dead?" one yelled. "Are you happy?" screamed another. "Are you running?" "How old are you?" "What happened to the eye?" "Is the governor going to make it?" "What happened back here?" "Where were you born?" "Who do you think has the mummy?"

I did not know what to do, so I just kept walking toward the car, shaking my head and pushing my way through them. It was a scene I had watched so many times on the evening news, when a person who had just done something to make news or was a big shot had to fight his way to his car. From the courtroom, from the scene of the murder, from the hospital, from the press conference, from the hearing, from the riot. Now here it was happening to me.

I finally got to the limo. The driver was excited to see me. He opened the back door of the car for me like I was royalty. There was somebody in there, sitting on the far side in the back. It scared me at first. He was a young man in a suit and tie.

"Rod Label wants you," he said, pointing his finger at me like he was Uncle Sam on the recruiting poster.

Rod Label was the famous host of *NightTalk with Rod Label,* a late-night network news program that featured hard-hitting interviews with people in the news. It came on in Oklahoma City at ten-thirty, right after the local news, and I watched it occasionally, whenever there was a hurricane, a hotel collapse or other major news event that I wanted to know more about.

I told the young man I had to go to the hospital to see my fallen governor.

"Rod does not take no for an answer, even from kings and prime ministers, sir," said the young man. "Here is a card with my name and number. I'll check back with you if you don't check back with me. Thank you. That was a great touch about the mummy, by the way. Rod said to tell you he loved it, too."

And he climbed out of the car after handing the limo driver what appeared to be a twenty-dollar bill.

"You ought to do it," said the driver, when he had closed the door and gone around to his position in the front seat. The window between the front and the back was down.

He said: "People would kill to get on *Rod Label.* Really kill. A guy asked me to give you this, too. It's from Joanne Mayer. Personally. The guy just ran it down from one of the booths."

I took a sealed envelope from him and opened it. Inside, in a beautiful handwriting, was the following note: "Mr. Lieutenant Governor, I would very much like to interview you on my program later this week. Thank you. Someone will call. Thank you." It was in fact signed by Joanne Mayer, a beautiful woman with long curly red hair who also interviewed people in the news on network television. She was particularly well known for a series of photographs of her in a light blue jumpsuit, leaning her head and red hair backward across chairs and things, that appeared in some national magazine. The jumpsuit was so tight-fitting you could see the outline of her underwear. The reporters in our press room at the capitol in Oklahoma City showed the pictures around and made fun of her as being more of a pinup than a reporter. But she was very famous, and I had heard somewhere that she was paid more than a million dollars a year, which I did not believe.

"You did great in that speech," said the chauffeur. "I was listening on the radio. I mean, you did great. Really great. I have never been with someone who has just made a speech like that. I have driven around a lot of celebrities. Frank Sinatra's daughter. What's her name? Nancy. Right, Nancy. Also, Bob Feller. Remember Rapid Robert? They called him Rapid Robert. He was in New York selling autographs."

He kept talking. "You are tremendous. You are going places. I take back what I said about politicians. I take it back. You're all right. Maybe it's the eye thing. What happened to it, by the way? I grew up with a guy in Queens who only had one thumb. The one on his right hand. His uncle whacked off the left one with a pair of those hedge scissors. You know, the ones with those teeth things on the blades. It was an accident. How about your eye?"

The car was moving.

"It just popped out one day," I said. Making up stories about my lost eye for strangers was one of my minor and harmless pleasures. I decided this guy deserved a big one. "Too much pressure built up in my brain, the doctors said. Like Coke in a bottle in the freezer. I tried to catch the eye with my hand when it popped out, but I missed the catch and it hit the floor and started rolling. My sister, hearing me scream, ran into the room and stepped on it by accident, squashed it and ruined it forever."

"To the hospital where they took your friend the governor, right, sir?" said the driver, who probably for the first time in his New York life was sorry he had asked.

He floorboarded us away from Madison Square Garden. And he wished me luck on finding the mummy and said he would personally keep a look out for it there in New York City. He said there were a lot of mummies walking the streets there, all right, and then he talked and talked about other things I do not remember.

I was doing everything I could to remember what I had just done at the Democratic National Convention before a television audience of eighty million people.

I was also dying to know what David Brinkley had said. The exact words.

6
. . .
THIS IS TODAY

I found them on the fifth floor of the hospital. Cal saw me walking down the hall and came trotting to meet me.

"Mack, my God a'mighty, Mack," he said. "Our one-eyed Oklahoma hero in person!"

He grabbed my right hand with both of his, like Speaker Andrews and, it seemed, all of the other people in my life did, and then gave me a bear hug.

"You made that speech like it was your own. My God a'mighty, you are something."

"Did Joe see it?"

"Not all of it, but a lot of it. He really liked the part about the mummy. So did I. Where did that come from?"

"Is he all right?"

"The mummy?"

"Joe."

"He's fine. They think a little blood vessel up there broke." He fingered a spot between his right ear and his neck. "But it'll mend. He's fine."

"Where is he? I can see him, can't I?"

It was then that I figured out Cal had been blocking my way from going on down the hall. And I noticed that he had, in fact, turned us back the other way, toward the elevator.

"He's sleeping now, Mack," Cal said. I could tell he was lying.

"What about Jill and the boys? I'd love to pay my respects to them. Are they sleeping, too?"

"No, but maybe tomorrow would be better."

We had arrived back at the elevator.

"What's the problem, Cal? Is he sicker than you are letting on, and you don't want me to know . . . ?"

He pushed the down button.

"He's fine. I told you he was fine. Just a little broken blood vessel."

"What is it, then, Cal?"

The elevator came and the door opened. Cal gave one of my elbows a gentle push. I stepped on, but I grabbed him and took him with me as the door closed.

"Hey, I need to stay here!"

"What's going on, Cal? I have a right to know, and you are now going to tell me."

The elevator stopped on the fourth floor. Two nurses got on. They ignored us. Cal put a finger to his mouth. Shut up, please, he was saying.

At the ground floor we walked to a small waiting room. There was nobody there.

"All right, Mack," Cal said in a quiet, concerned voice. "Joe did see your speech. He loved it. You did it beautifully. He couldn't talk, but it was clear he was so proud and excited with the way you did it. But then Brinkley said what he said and . . . well, it threw him into some kind of fit. They had to sedate him and run him through some more tests. It turned into a real emergency. We thought he might really die this time. Jill gave orders that you are never to set eyes on Joe again. She'll get over it, but that's the way it is for now."

"What did Brinkley actually say? I know the general thing, but that's all."

Cal sighed. "Well. Right after you finished your speech and the people were cheering and clapping and all, Chancellor turned to Brinkley and said something about wondering who Senator Griffin would now consider for his running mate if he still wanted to go with a southern strategy. Now that Governor Hayman was apparently out of the running. Brinkley said, 'What about him?' He motioned with his head to the podium. 'At least for the Short List. The country could do with a national candidate with a search for a mummy as a priority.' He meant you, of course. He was talking about you. I guess the idea of his losing his own place in the sun, even to you, was not a great thing to Joe. So that's why I think it would not do well to see him and Jill and the boys tonight. Let's have breakfast at the hotel in the morning."

I had the limo driver take me back to the Claremont.

"You're it tonight," he said. "It. I-T, it. On every station, on every call-in you are it. The one-eyed guy with the mummy story. That's what they're talking about. I just heard some guy call in from California, where else, saying he saw a mummy the other day down the street from him in a park. The host talked him up about it and it turned out it was at a wax museum. You are going to bring them out of the closet. Yes, sir. Out of the closet they are going to come running to you. Yes, sir."

There were five or six reporters, two with hand-held TV cameras, waiting for me in the lobby of the Claremont.

"Any leads on the mummy yet?" one of them yelled at me.

"Not yet," I replied with a pleasant Oklahoma smile.

"Are you going to release your income tax returns?" another screamed.

My income tax returns? I kept walking toward the elevator.

"Brinkley says you're on the Short List," said another. "Is that true?"

I pushed the elevator up button. And shook my head and smiled. The journalists crowded around me. I felt a camera in my ribs. A young woman with black hair that needed combing, and garlic on her breath, said, "Are you owned by Big Oil?"

I shook my head and smiled.

"How did you lose the left eye?" someone else with a female voice shrieked.

The elevator came and I waved good-bye to the group of journalists. I wondered how they trained for such work, how much they were paid, what their mothers and fathers thought of what they did for a living.

There was a woman waiting for me in front of the door to my hotel room. She was at least sixty years old and was dressed in a long red and yellow dress that went down to the floor. Her head was wrapped in a turban of the same cloth as the dress was made of. The turban and the dress were spotted with stains of what looked and smelled like grease and food, and I wondered if she had just shared dinner with that woman reporter downstairs.

"I am Madame Mishara Van Looy," she said, exposing the fact that two of her teeth right in front were missing and two others were capped with gold. "I am the world's foremost communicator with the dead and gone. I spoke a few moments ago with Mr. Booth."

"Mr. Booth?" I said.

"John Wilkes Booth, the man you referred to in your speech. I told him your story and asked if it was true. He said it was not true. He said he died in a tobacco farm fire in Virginia after the assassination of President Lincoln. He said the man who died in Oklahoma and who was mummified was an impostor. He expressed shock and outrage and asked that I intervene with you on his behalf. That is why I am here. He told me you could be reached at the Claremont Hotel, and he gave me your room number. I am not crazy, Mr. Lieutenant Governor Mack, and if you think I am, then that makes you the crazy one."

"I am sorry to hear Mr. Booth is upset," was all I could think to say.

"For five hundred dollars I will not reveal this information to anyone other than you."

"Forget it, ma'am," I said, moving my key toward the lock on my room door.

"Three-fifty?" she said.

"Please stand aside," I said.

"One hundred. That is my final offer."

"Please!"

I opened the door and walked in, as she said, "You will regret this decision, Mr. Mack. You will regret it."

I went directly to the twenty-four-hour room service menu. It was going to cost twenty-five dollars by the time the service charge and the tip were added in, but I figured so what, and dialed 2 and ordered a tunafish-salad sandwich on toasted wheat bread, an order of fries, a Diet Pepsi and a piece of hot apple pie with a slice of melted cheddar cheese. I figured I had earned something special for what I had done and been through tonight. What do you think about that, Mr. Booth?

I called home while I waited for the food.

Jackie had seen it all on television. And loved it. I assured her Joe was going to be all right. That made it possible for her to be even happier. I think.

"I can't believe David Brinkley said that about you being vice-president!"

"There's never been a one-eyed vice-presidential candidate, and there never will be," said I.

"You'll take it if it's offered, won't you, Mack?"

"Sure. And I'll take the popeship and the king-of-England-ship and the largest Cadillac dealership in Tulsa if they're offered, too."

"Where did Joe get that mummy story?" she asked. "I think you would have done well to have left that out. You were under no obligation to say everything that fool had in his speech."

I almost said something but decided against it. We went on to talk about less important things, and then she came back to my night in the sun.

"You know, Mack, I got a call from Hammerschmidt right after you spoke," she said. "He wondered why, with you making the speech yourself, you didn't put in his line about turning the post office over to private enterprise and all the rest? That would sure have made more sense than that mummy business."

I wanted very much to slam that phone down as hard as I could. But I didn't. I just told her I had missed what she had said because somebody was knocking at the door. It must be room service with my dinner, I said.

Good-bye for now, I said.

And she told me again how great I had been, even with the mummy thing.

• • •

Next came the first time I had ever tried to go to sleep after being mentioned by David Brinkley as a possibility for a vice-presidential Short List.

Lying in the magnificent king-sized bed in that magnificent hotel suite, I first played back my magnificent performance on that podium at Madison Square Garden. I imagined picking up the phone, calling David Brinkley and saying, David, hi, this is The One-Eyed Mack from Oklahoma. I hope I didn't wake you. But I am calling to thank you personally for what you said about me tonight, and would you mind saying it again for me exactly the way you said it to America?

I tried to imagine what it would be like to be the Democratic nominee for vice-president of the United States. It didn't work. Nothing much would come into focus, because I had no idea what it was like to be such a thing. It was one thing to be the Second Man of Oklahoma but quite another to be the Second Man of all of America!

I tried to think of what it would be like actually to be the vice-president of the United States. What exactly does he do? I knew about presiding over the U.S. Senate and waiting around for the president to die. But what else? When does he go to work in the morning? Where does he go to work? How many people work for him? What do they do for him? Where does he live? I thought I remembered reading somewhere that there was a house the government owned for vice-presidents. I wondered what ever had happened to Spiro Agnew. Had he been on a Short List? I knew vice-presidents went to a lot of funerals. No problem there. I did a lot of that as lieutenant governor of Oklahoma. Does he have a limo? With a TV? How many Secret Service agent bodyguards are around him? Does he have to send things out to the cleaners and the laundry? Does he go out to get a haircut, or does the barber come to him? Can he walk around by himself outside? What are the rules for vice-presidents going to drive-thru restaurants?

I went through my conversation with Jackie another eight or nine times. Here am I, her husband, on my night of nights like no night ever before in my life or ninety-nine percent of all other people's lives, and she wants to know why I did not throw in some stupid line about some crazy Trailways man's crazy idea about turning the nation's post offices into bus stations and drive-thru groceries—or vice versa and whatever!

I wished very much that I had told her the truth about the mummy. But she didn't really give me a chance.

I thought about trying to find Cal to ask him for another Valium, but the next thing I knew the phone was ringing me out of a dead sleep.

There was a digital clock by the phone on the bedside table. It said it was four thirty-five in the morning.

A female voice said to me:

"This is Nancy Ryan of *The CBS Morning News.* I hope I didn't wake you. I was calling to see if you would be available to appear on our program this morning. We will send a car for you at six-thirty. Hughes Rudd will be asking the questions. You have become quite a star because of your speech and the reaction. Maybe on the Short List? Hughes will ask you about that. Also about the story in the *Times* this morning about your oilman friend."

The CBS Morning News? They want me on the *The CBS Morning News?* Hughes Rudd? Oilman friend? What story?

I woke up enough to remember what Cal had said about Joe the night before. Seeing me on *The CBS Morning News* might mean instant death for Joe Hayman of Buffalo, Oklahoma.

"Thank you, but no. I cannot be with you this morning. Please pass on my regrets to Mr. Rudd. What oilman friend story?"

"You haven't seen the *Times*?"

"No ma'am. I have been asleep."

"It's about the man on whose plane you flew up here. He's a convicted swindler, I believe. Did *Today* or *GMA* get to you first?"

I hung up.

The CBS Morning News. With Hughes Rudd. Easy come, easy go. What did the *Times* say about Cal? What *Times*?

The phone rang again.

It was a female voice from *Good Morning America* on ABC, promising questions from David Hartman!

Same thing, same pitch. "Were you involved with this Mr. Blackwell in the slanted-oil-well enterprise?" she said. "David will want to know."

I said no, thank you, and hung up, and almost immediately there was a call from a male voice inviting me to appear on *Today,* Oklahoma's favorite television program. That was because of Jim Hartz and Frank McGee.

"Jim Hartz wanted me to personally ask you, as one Oklahoman to another," said the voice. "He said to say 'Boomer Sooner,' and that you would know what that meant. He said if that didn't work, then say 'Crown Oklahoma.'"

Jim Hartz had been born and raised in Tulsa, and he was proud of it. He had followed in the footsteps of Frank McGee, another Oklahoman, as the top man on that early-morning program. I had met Jim Hartz a couple of times when he had been home emceeing dinners or making speeches, but it would be too much to say that we were friends—acquaintances, even.

The next thing I knew, I had agreed to be picked up by a limousine at six twenty-five. I also called the hotel operator and told her to start taking phone messages from reporters and people like that, instead of just automatically connecting them to the room.

I waited an hour and then woke up Cal to tell him I was going to be on *Today,* and could he please make sure Joe did not watch it. He said he could.

"There's a story in a newspaper about you," I said to him finally.

"I just read it. It's not a good one. I am sorry, Mack. The last thing in the world I would ever want is to hurt you or Joe in any way. All of that slant-well stuff was so long ago I can't believe anyone would think it's important now."

"Well, it's not important," I said, more out of hope than conviction.

"Good luck on the *Today* show, Mack. I was just on the phone to back home. You are a real hit back there. A God-a'mighty ding-dong hit. Every Oklahoma newspaper and TV station has great things to say about our one-eyed lieutenant governor of Oklahoma going to the rescue of his governor and a mummy. I'm going to try to keep that news from Joe, too. It'd cause every blood vessel in his skull to pop."

The *Today* show was broadcast from the fifth floor of the same building where Radio City Music Hall was located. So at least I got to see the outside of it on the way to my interview with Jim Hartz.

I was first taken to what was called a Green Room, which had coffee and rolls and doughnuts but wasn't green, and then to a makeup room to have powder and goo smeared on my face. There were copies of *The New York Times* everywhere, and I saw a headline that said:

DEM KEYNOTER
HAS CLOSE TIES
TO OIL FELON

FLEW TO NEW YORK ON PLANE

OILMAN ADMITTED ROLE
IN SLANT OIL WELL SCANDAL

I did not read the story. I decided to follow an old precept of Buffalo Joe's. "You can't answer a lot of questions about stories you haven't read, Mack," he said to me one day when *The Daily Oklahoman* ran a blast over one of his appointees to the State Turnpike Authority Board. "And there ain't nobody in the world who can make you read something you don't want to read. Remember that, Mack."

I remembered it.

The interview was done at a desk, with Jim Hartz and me looking at each other from angles. I wondered why they did it that way. Why not have the interviewer and the one being interviewed sit across from one another so they could have direct eye contact? Why sit at an angle like that?

Jim Hartz was very nice to me, and he said he remembered me from the Oklahoma Oilman of the Year dinner two years before in Lawton. His introduction was beautiful. It mentioned my having started in politics as a county commissioner and Jackie's success as the founder of JackieMarts.

The interview itself? Well, here is an exact transcript that I reprint with the permission of NBC:

HARTZ: First, I hope my journalistic peers will excuse my saying right at the beginning, Congratulations. You made all Oklahomans proud last night, Mr. Lieutenant Governor.

L.G.: Thank you. We have always been very proud of you, too, Jim.

HARTZ: Thank you. And my mother in Tulsa thanks you.

L.G.: Great, Jim. Great.

HARTZ: Can you give us an update on how Governor Hayman is doing?

L.G.: He is out of danger and resting comfortably.

HARTZ: Well, if you would pass on to him my concerns and those of all Americans, I would certainly appreciate it. Maybe he's watching us now. If he is, then the job has just been done.

L.G.: I will certainly tell him, if he did not hear it himself.

HARTZ: Thank you. Now to some business, if we may, sir. I assume you have seen the story in *The New York Times* this morning about Cal Blackwell?

L.G.: No, I haven't.

HARTZ: Right. Right. Well, the upshot of the story is that Cal Blackwell, who was convicted of fraud and swindling in the slant oil-well scandal of the 1960s, has a close relationship with you and Governor Hayman. You and the governor flew up here on his private plane, even. A slant oil well, for those who do not know, being a well that is not drilled straight down, but at an angle, in order to steal a neighbor's oil. Can I get your reaction?

L.G.: It is an awful thing Cal Blackwell did, Jim, no question about it. But he admitted his mistake, and he went before a judge and took his medicine. That was over ten years ago and he has gone on to become a constructive force in the petroleum industry and in affairs of our Sooner State.

HARTZ: What about the airplane rides?

L.G.: What about them? Cal's a friend of Governor Hayman and the State of Oklahoma. Would it be all right if he drove us in his pickup to the grocery store to buy some soda? It's the same thing. That's what friends do in Oklahoma, Jim, as you know. They give each other rides and do things together. What's wrong with that?

HARTZ: Have you or Governor Hayman ever done any favors there within your state government for Cal Blackwell?

L.G.: Certainly not.

HARTZ: Has he ever given you any expensive gifts?

L.G.: No.

HARTZ: What about his Packard car collection? Everyone in Oklahoma knows about it and the *Times* mentions it. He owns 147 blue 1948 Packards. Some people find that strange, I guess.

L.G.: Well, like I say, I haven't read the story, but I would say that Cal Blackwell, just like every other citizen of the United States of America, has the right to collect anything his desires and finances can handle. I am sure John Hancock and the others certainly had Free Choice of Hobbies in mind when they declared their independence from Britain and established this country. I know, and you know, our State of Oklahoma has always believed in a Free Choice of Hobbies for one and all.

HARTZ: What about your name? AP is reporting that you changed your name to Mack. That your real name is Donald. Is that true?

L.G.: Yes, sir. Mack as in truck.

HARTZ: Why did you change your name?

L.G.: Wouldn't you prefer Mack as in truck to Donald as in duck?

HARTZ: Well, yes, I guess I would. What do you think your chances are of being picked for the ticket?

L.G.: I think my chances are very slim. One-eyed lieutenant governors of Oklahoma don't bring a lot of constituencies to a ticket, Jim.

HARTZ: Are you in fact on the Short List?

L.G.: If I am, then I don't know it. I think only your wonderful NBC man David Brinkley has talked about that possibility so far.

HARTZ: Well, good luck, sir.

L.G.: Thank you. Same to you, Jim. Be sure and stop by the capitol the next time you're home.

HARTZ: Yes, sir. Right. I will sure do that. I can't end this without asking if there has been any luck yet in the search for the John Wilkes Booth mummy.

L.G.: Not that I know of. Thanks for asking.

HARTZ: Some of the skeptics around here were wondering this morning if all of that was a put-on. It's not, is it, Mr. Lieutenant Governor?

L.G.: Certainly not, Jim. Certainly not. It's all right there in the papers and the history books for everyone to read.

HARTZ: That's what I told them. Thanks again for being with us. This is *Today* on NBC.

Cal was waiting for me in the lobby of the Claremont. He looked like he needed some of his own Valium. Off in the corner as we sat in two chairs between two large potted trees, he said to me in a frantic half-whisper:

"You were great, Mack. You were great. You were really great. But we have a problem. I mean a real problem. A friend who handles my car business just called me. You told Hartz that I had never given you any gifts. Which was true as far as you knew. But it isn't technically true anymore, as of a few minutes ago. You remember that call about the 1957 Ford Fairlanes? Well, I went ahead and bought them and said to deliver them to your house in Oklahoma City, as a kind of surprise gift from me. You know, to be that starter in a collection, like I was talking about. Well, they expedited everything and put them on a truck last night in Arkansas and sent them right over overnight. My guy says they did just what I told them to do. They unloaded them in front of your house and tied a huge, I mean huge, ribbon around them, with a huge card from me. Well, I could have them picked up right away and taken away, but unfortunately there were a bunch of reporters and photographers at your house this morning to do a story about you, the Great Keynoter, and your wife...."

At that precise moment, a young man in a hotel uniform walked up to us.

"Mr. Lieutenant Governor, I am sorry to interrupt, but

there is an urgent telephone call for you. It is from Senator Griffin."

"Oh my God," I said, and followed him to a private office.

Senator Griffin introduced himself on the phone and then asked if I could have breakfast with him at his hotel. He said a car could be there to pick me up in five minutes.

I said I would be ready.

Cal waited with me in the lobby the five minutes. He mostly said how sorry he was. I mostly said nothing, because I had no idea what to say to him or to anyone else about anything.

7

. . .

KICK THE CAN

Senator Daniel Michael Griffin's traits and peculiarities were well known to me and all other Americans who read newspapers and magazines and watched the news on television. He was tall, red-faced, brilliant, articulate, funny, liberal, Irish, Catholic and strange. He had entered the race for the Democratic nomination as a long shot, as somebody given no chance to do more than raise a few of his favorite issues and then disappear shortly after the New Hampshire primary. But he had surprised everyone by turning his full energies first to the early caucuses in Iowa, which the other candidates had mostly ignored until it was too late. He'd charmed those Iowa farmers into thinking he was one of them, even though he was from New Jersey, and he'd gone on to win New Hampshire and to wrap up the nomination in Wisconsin. There had been seven candidates in the race with him when he'd started; only two, Jimmy Carter and Morris Udall, were there when it ended.

I walked into Daniel Michael Griffin's suite at a hotel called the Pierre expecting to have a special, memorable experience, and that was exactly what happened.

"Do you want a bowl of soup, too?" were the first words out of his mouth. He came through the doorway to a huge sitting room toward me. His suite was even bigger than mine. To our left was a giant picture window that looked out dead west across Central Park.

His right hand was sticking rigidly out in front of him like a tiller in front of a tractor.

"I eat tomato cream soup for breakfast," he said, as he arrived and took hold of my right hand. "What about you?"

"I'll pass," I said.

"What is the native breakfast of Oklahoma?" He motioned for me to have a seat in a chair on one side of a small dining room table.

I looked down at the food that somebody had already ordered for me. There was half of a green-colored melon, some barely cooked bacon, two pieces of white-bread toast, a glass of orange juice, and coffee. "This is fine," I said.

"That wasn't the question, though, was it? What kind of breakfasts do the native people of Oklahoma eat?"

"The real natives are Indians. They eat mostly maize flakes and barbecued squirrel. With the rest of us, it just depends on where we live. People in southern Oklahoma eat mostly shortstacks and sausage. Northern Oklahoma, it's pecan waffles and ham. Central Oklahoma, only watery scrambled eggs and Wheaties..."

It was a smart-mouth answer and it just sprang out of my mouth, like that story I had told the limousine driver about my eye popping out.

Griffin grinned, picked up his glass of orange juice and

held it up and at me. I grabbed my glass of orange juice. We clinked our glasses together.

"I like you, sir," he said. "I like your style. On the *Today* show a while ago, last night on that podium—my God, you were good. I like that simplicity of yours. 'Mack as in truck.' Well, well." He dragged out the second "well" like it was two syllables. Well-luh. He pronounced most syllables of most words like they were important. "Your words last night were superb. Truly superb." Superb-buh.

"They were Governor Hayman's words. I merely recited them."

"That's what we politicians do, recite other people's words. It's the recitation that matters. All that matters. Speeches are emotional not intellectual exercises. People hear a speech and remember if they cried or laughed, but not what it was that caused them to do either or both. I haven't written one of my own speeches in twenty years. It is a waste of my time. I concentrate on the delivery. Great writers are common. Great deliverers are rare. Tell me who you are. I am as intrigued as the rest of America is this morning."

I looked at him carefully. I decided he was serious. So I gave him a serious and complete answer. I told him about being born in Kansas, the son of a Kansas highway patrolman and a wonderful woman he loved very much who had died of appendicitis with a 107-degree temperature when I was twelve. I told him about graduating from junior college and emigrating to Oklahoma, where I had married a widow and became a county commissioner and then ended up lieutenant governor.

"What about the war? Why did you leave that out?"

"I was alive during World War Two and the Korean and the Vietnam wars. . . ."

He put a finger up to his left eye. "I meant your being decorated for valor in Korea when you lost your eye. The papers this morning said that was the story."

"That was my widow wife's husband, Pepper. He fell on a hand grenade. We were all friends. Jackie and I married after he died."

"Then how did you lose the eye?" I could tell he was disappointed I wasn't a war hero. Most people were. Particularly people in politics. I decided this was not the time or the place to tell a wild lost-eye story and Senator Griffin was not the person to tell one to.

"I was watching some kids play kick-the-can, and the can got kicked up in my eye and tore it out," I said truthfully.

"What's kick-the-can?"

I put down my fork and shook my head like I had never in my life heard anything so startling.

"What is the matter, Mack?" said Senator Griffin. He was now pronouncing Mack "Mack-kuh."

"Sorry, Senator. But I think the people in my part of the country would wonder how in the world a man who doesn't know about kick-the-can could possibly be president of the United States."

That stiffened him. He shoved himself back from the table and shot himself up. Up to about six-five or so.

"Show me, sir. Demonstrate."

"Kick-the-can?"

"Exactly, sir. Exactly-uh."

I got up and looked around the room. There were expensive glass ashtrays and telephones with twenty-five buttons, and lamps and lampshades and chairs and things. But no tin cans. Our orange juice glasses might break.

Then I had an idea. "Where's the bathroom?"

He pointed toward a door. "Right through there. But don't take all day. This is a busy day for me...."

I went into the bathroom, removed the roll of toilet paper from the dispenser and returned to Senator Griffin.

"This will play the part of a tin can," I said. "I will place it here in the middle of the room. Got it?"

"Got it."

"Now, for purposes of demonstration, I will be It. I will now close my eye and count to ten. Out loud. You will go and hide. But hide in such a way that you could run across and kick the can, or in this case the toilet paper, before I tag you...."

The tall, thin man looked at me and the toilet paper and let out one of the wildest laughs I had ever heard.

Then he said: "Here I am, on the threshold of being nominated as the Democratic candidate for president of the United States, a position often called that of leader of the Free World-duh. And what am I doing? I am on the threshold of kicking a roll of toilet paper about a room on the eighteenth floor of the Pierre Hotel-luh."

He walked over and kicked that roll of toilet paper with his right foot. The roll sailed up against the picture window and fell harmlessly to the floor.

"Mack, I'm putting you on the Short List for vice-president. There are four others already on it. Lyman of Maine, Adair of Illinois, Carter of Georgia and Manning of California. Now there's Mack of Oklahoma."

"Oh no, not me. Governor Hayman is the one you want. He's well on the road to recovery now...."

"If I end up asking you to join me on the ticket, will you accept?"

"Well, I don't know. It might kill Joe. I mean it, seriously. It might kill him."

"Do not worry about Joe Hayman. We politicians can survive disappointment and defeat. We, in fact, are the only group of people in American society who are trained to survive disappointment and defeat. Joe Hayman will cry, Joe Hayman will bleed, and Joe Hayman will hate, but he will not die."

"You're not concerned about the oilman story this morning?"

"Should I be?"

"No, sir."

"It's all in the handling, Mack. You handled it beautifully this morning on *Today*. John Vickers of my staff will be in touch with your staff. We'll have to run some checks on you and he'll have to ask you some stupid questions. The Eagleton legacy demands it. I have also asked Richardson McKinney to have some words with you about more substantial matters. I hope you do not mind that, either."

"Not at all, sir," I said. Richardson McKinney was one of the most famous Democratic presidential insiders of all time.

Griffin said: "Thursday morning I will be calling everyone on the Short List to tell them my decision. Good hunting."

Good hunting? My staff? Richardson McKinney?

He stuck that long right arm of his at me one more time. And we shook hands.

"Look, it's probably crazy suddenly to put somebody on the Short List like this," he said. "But everybody already knows I'm crazy-uh. Do you really believe somebody's sitting out there in this nation of ours with the mummy of John Wilkes Booth stashed in his attic?"

"Maybe. Our historical society thinks so."

"Well, Mack, let me make you a promise. If I am elected president of the United States, if the people of this great land choose me to lead the greatest and most powerful nation on the face of this earth, I will put the full force of the Federal Bureau of Investigation, the Central Intelligence Agency, the Bureau of Mines and whatever else it takes to find that mummy of yours. That sir, is my solemn word, and I never, ever go back on my solemn word, so help me God."

He shook my right hand and left the room through the doorway he had entered many monumental minutes before.

"Surprise!"

And there she was. Jackie, my incredible wife, standing there all beautiful and smart in the middle of my beautiful and smart hotel suite. I had just returned from one of the most miserable experiences of my life—the interview with Senator Griffin's man John Vickers.

Jackie and I hugged each other tightly, like we had been in different worlds for many months. She said she had decided right then and there as she was watching me on the *Today* show that she would come to New York to be with me in my hours of incredible need. She had immediately thrown some things into a suitcase and headed for the Will Rogers, our airport in Oklahoma City.

"To hell with privatizing the post offices," she said as we hugged. She didn't often use "hell" like that as a cuss word. She seldom cussed at all, in fact. Few Oklahoma women did, except in Tulsa and near the Arkansas border.

We sat down on one of the two couches in the room. I told her about my strange and wonderful time with Senator Daniel Michael Griffin of New Jersey.

And then I recounted my several awful minutes with John Vickers.

I reminded her that as a category of Person, few were

worse than Top Aide to a Very Important Person. Back at the courthouse in Adabel, Oklahoma, where I had begun my career in the service of the public, the scabbiest, most difficult person had been the chief deputy sheriff. Second had been the chief deputy county clerk. The executive assistant district attorney had been third. All three people had loved to pick at people for no reason when they came to pay a bond, duplicate a document or whatever, just to show they could do it.

John Vickers, Senator Griffin's Top Aide, was a triple-A example of the category.

"Are you a homosexual?" was his first question.

"No," I replied.

"Is there anyone who thinks you are a homosexual who might say so publicly?"

"No."

Vickers resembled the walrus at the Oklahoma City Zoo. He wore his black hair lacquered and combed straight back. He was about my height, which is five feet ten, but he carried at least 250 pounds, most of which was in layers of rolling skin from the chin on down. He was sitting at the head of a long conference table on the fifty-third floor of an office building around the corner from the Claremont. The message from the senator's office had said I was free to bring my Top Aide. I had no such thing. I had thought about asking Cal but decided against it and then hated myself for doing so. So I was alone, sitting at the table at Vickers's left. He was hunched down with a yellow legal pad in front of him. He was left-handed, and he curled up his hand in a circle like he was coming at the paper upside down.

His eyes were barely open, like he was barely able to keep from falling asleep.

"Are you engaged in any illicit sexual activities with any person of either sex?"

"No."

"Are there any sexual matters of any kind in your present or past that if known might cause you and the senator problems?"

"No."

"Have you ever been treated for mental illness?"

"No."

"No shock treatments for depression or anything like that?"

"No."

"No conversations on a professional basis with a psychiatrist, psychologist or professional counselor of any kind?"

"No."

"Do you belong to any private clubs or country clubs that discriminate against blacks, women or Jews?"

"No."

The Walrus looked up from his paper. "You sure?"

"I don't play golf."

"Oh." Back to his notes. "Have you ever taken a bribe?"

"No."

"Have you ever committed a crime?"

"No."

"Ever been charged, indicted, convicted, jailed or publicly accused of a crime?"

"No."

"Do you have a drinking problem?"

"No."

"Do you take or traffic in drugs?"

"No."

"Describe your financial condition."

"Fine."

"Anybody or company have financial control over you?"

"No."

"Describe your medical condition."

"Excellent."

"What is your religion?"

"Church of the Holy Road."

"What's that?"

"Fundamentalist Protestant."

"Tongues?"

"No."

"Born again?"

"Yes."

"Kooky?"

"No."

"How would you describe your political philosophy?"

"Oklahoma moderate."

"What's that?"

"Like Texas conservative, only more so."

"Are any members of your family in a position to embarrass you, either through past acts or accusations or revelations about their conduct or yours?"

"No."

"Your father's occupation?"

"Kansas state highway patrolman."

"Mother's occupation, if any?"

"She is gone now, but she was a secretary until she married my dad."

"Was what you said on the *Today* show about this Cal Blackwell all there is to say?"

"Yes. He's more Governor Hayman's friend than mine."

"You sure?"

"Yes."

"Is there anything in your past or present that if known could hurt your candidacy for vice-president of the United States?"

"No."

"Thank you. That's it. The vice-presidential acceptance speech is being written now by one of our people. If you are chosen, a copy will be sent to you immediately."

"What if I want to write my own speech?"

That got The Walrus to raise his eyes and look at me.

"We'll take care of it," he said.

"How can you write a speech for someone before that someone is even chosen?"

"It's the way it's done," he said.

I repeated this all to Jackie. "Then he dismissed me like I was with room service at this hotel," I said. "If I do end up vice-president I am going to remember him."

My own words made me laugh: "If I do end up vice-president . . ."

Jackie had gotten up from the couch and gone over to her purse, which was in the bedroom. She returned now with a white envelope.

"Your friend C. caught me at the airport before I left. He came driving up with a police escort, lights, sirens, everything. He said to give you this. He said he did not want to do any talking about it on the telephone because of what he called security reasons."

I took the envelope and pulled out a single piece of white stationery. It was a note in his handwriting.

Mack—

I was watching you this morning on the TV. The business about Cal Blackwell is a bigger problem than you know. Yesterday afternoon the narcotics people of the Oklahoma PD pulled the plug on one of their exes who had been dealing. He's been singing in order to make a deal. He's singing names of customers. One of the names they have is Blackwell. I can keep a lid on it for a while. But be careful and stay off his airplanes!

I can't wait to tell you about the Pickled Pig case down in Purcell. Two pig farmers got into it, over firing the preacher at their Baptist church. One started feeding the other one's pigs whiskey.

Good luck on the vice-president thing. Everybody is pulling for you and the mummy.

C.

I read it to Jackie and then asked, "What else can happen?"

"Do you know about the five cars?"

I told her I did.

But that did not prevent her from describing in detail the scene in front of the house when she had looked out and seen a truck with five old cars on it and a gigantic red ribbon around them being photographed by television cameramen.

We both laughed when she was through, and I again asked, "What else can happen?"

Richardson McKinney, advisor to presidents, was everything in person he should have been. And then some. Vickers had reminded me like I was stupid that Mr. McKinney had been one of Roosevelt's young warriors and a confidant of Truman's, and I already knew that he had served in the cabinet of Presidents Kennedy and Johnson. Now here he was having lunch with me. Just the two of us at a French restaurant near the hotel. I do not remember the exact name but it was Le Something-or-other that meant "snail" or "turtle." The Snail or The Turtle. I had been to France once in my life, but that was only for a short time solely to try to get the speaker of our Oklahoma House of Representatives to come home. He had run away with some old buddies from the Marine Corps to see if they could recapture a life they had had twenty-five years before. Our speaker, Luther Wallace, would not come back and still had not come back. But that is another whole story.

"I took the liberty of ordering for both of us," Mr. McKinney said after we sat down. "I hope you don't mind. That way we will not be disturbed except for the service." Where we sat down was not out in the public open. It was in a small room with a table and chairs, surrounded by racks of wine. We were the only people there.

I told him I did not mind.

"I ordered us both the grouper," he said. "It is their specialty. They poach it and serve it in a special sauce; the recipe has been handed down from father to son chefs since 1745."

"Sounds great," I said. I had never heard of any food called grouper. Was it a kind of beef? Like veal? A special East Coast or French way of cooking chicken? Maybe it was a casserole of some kind. I hoped and prayed it was not liver or fish. I hated all liver and all fish except tuna in a salad.

"The sommelier recommended a 1971 Meursault," said Mr. McKinney.

I was not expected to respond, and I didn't. "Sommelier" was pronounced "some'll-*yea*." I had no idea who or what it was. A 1971 Meursault? McKinney had sent over a driver and a 1976 Cadillac limousine to pick me up. I had no idea what a Meursault car looked like or even what country made it.

First there was a soup. It was orange and tasted like a

carrot. I assumed it was carrot soup, something I did not know existed until that very second I put the first sip into my mouth.

A man came with a bottle of wine. I declined, because I do not drink alcohol of any kind. Mr. McKinney was surprised but pleased.

"Is your abstinence founded on a religious belief?" he asked.

"No, sir," I replied "It makes me sick."

Richardson McKinney had dark brown eyes, and dark gray hair that was a series of waves across the top of his head. He wore a dark blue suit with slight light blue stripes that looked like it had been pressed seconds before he had come to the restaurant. His shirt was white and had cuffs that folded up with cuff links. I knew of no other person who wore shirts with cuff links on an everyday basis. I assumed having lunch with people like me was less than an everyday thing to him.

His voice was solid, shined wood. Slick, deep and dark. I could not imagine him saying "uh" or "you know" or even "well." All of his sentences began and ended like all English teachers at all grades wanted all sentences to begin and end.

"The Senator has asked me to speak to you about your views on what this nation and this world face as we enter the end of the decade of the seventies and head for the eighties," he said. "He's asked me to get a feel for your mind, your positions and ideas on the issues. That is, after all, what elections are all about. Do you not agree?"

I agreed.

"Let me also say right here at the beginning that I consider this conversation to be completely and forever off the record. Neither one of us will talk of it with anyone other than Senator Griffin, now or ever. I assume that is suitable to you?"

"Yes, sir," I said.

"Can we include our respective memoirs in that ban?"

"Yes, sir." The idea of my ever writing any memoirs was a joke, but as far as he was concerned it was not. Richardson McKinney may have already done a couple, for all I knew.

"How do you feel about the seventies, Mr. Lieutenant Governor?" he asked. And the interview was on.

" 'Mack,' please. Everyone calls me Mack. Well, about the seventies. To tell you the truth, I have never sat down and thought about the whole ten years like that. I have not said to myself, Look here now, what do you think about this ten-year set as compared to the last one or the next one?"

"I see," he said. He looked me right in my good eye, smiled like he was my grandfather, which he was more than old enough to be, and took another sip of his soup. He took his sips, by the way, with his soup spoon moving from the front of the bowl to the back. The way I had been taught to do it and did it was the opposite: start at the back and scoop toward the front.

"Is this the time to move aggressively for arms control agreements with the Soviets, Mr. Lieutenant Governor?" he asked.

"To tell you the truth, that is just not my area of expertise," I replied.

"Are the multiwarhead limits ever going to be effective?"

"Like I say, that is simply not my thing."

"What if the Russians continue to refuse to count their Backfire bombers?"

"Can't help you on that, sir. Sorry."

He asked me a couple more questions about nuclear weapons and then said: "The Osprey. What is your position on the Osprey?"

"It's not something I know anything about."

"The Osprey is an airplane that the Marine Corps wants," said Richardson McKinney. "It rises straight up like a helicopter and then can fly away like a regular airplane."

"My best friend and wife's first husband was a Marine."

"So you would support the concept of the Osprey's use?"

"I do not know anything about that, Mr. McKinney. Nothing at all."

The main course was served. Grouper was fish, the very worst kind. A fishy fish, the exact type that I not only did not eat, I did not like even to be in the same room with. But I cut little pieces off and began sticking them in my mouth like they were dissolvable pills. I swallowed them whole, without chewing, with them only barely and quickly even touching the inside of my mouth.

Mr. McKinney moved the discussion to another area of international relations.

"What is your position on aiding the democratic resistance of Nicaragua?" he asked.

Nicaragua. I looked down at my grouper and tried to sort it out. But I couldn't. So I said: "To tell you the truth, Mr. McKinney, I can never keep Nicaragua and El Salvador apart. One is run by leftists with death squads and the other is run by rightists with death squads. I can't ever remember which is a democratic resistance and which isn't, which we are supporting and which we aren't. I'm sorry. Sometimes I get them both mixed up with Guatemala. Or Puerto Rico. But I know Puerto Rico is wrong, because I noticed they send delegates to the Democratic convention. Sorry. My views are not fully formed on this issue."

Richardson McKinney was amused. He smiled, and for a minute I thought he might even laugh. I knew if he did laugh it would be at me not with me. I was coming over as an empty-headed hick from Oklahoma. I knew it, but there was nothing I could do about it. Maybe that's what I was?

He changed to economics. "Are wage and price controls good for the country?" he asked.

"I really am not an expert on that," I said. "I guess there could be times like when there's a war that you need to do things like that. Otherwise, forget it."

"How do we deal with OPEC?"

"Oh-what?"

"OPEC, the oil cartel."

I shook my head and said honestly, "I have no idea. I really do not."

"Do you have an economic philosophy?"

"No, sir."

"Is there an economist or economic theorist whose views most represent yours?"

"No, sir."

"How much control should the federal government exert over the marketplace?"

"I am really not qualified to say."

He was pausing between questions to take and chew and thoroughly enjoy bites of his grouper. He also, it seemed to me, got warmer and friendlier and happier with each question and each non-answer. Which was a mystery, because it seemed clear to me that if this was the oral exam to be the Democratic nominee for vice-president, I was failing. And failing miserably. Why was he so happy? Was he pulling for somebody else on the Short List?

We went on to immigration policy, the line-item veto, health care for the elderly, China, the Panama Canal, human rights and several other things. I had something to say about gun control and providing good health care for everyone in the country, but other than that he drew mostly blanks. By the time we got through the salad to the dessert, a mushy kind of custard thing that tasted like burnt almond, in a tall, thin glass bowl, I was sure that my chances of being chosen as Senator Griffin's running mate had ended. Period.

By the time we got to coffee I knew it for certain. And I said so to Mr. McKinney. "I am sorry you have wasted your time," I said. "Clearly Senator Griffin was operating on a spur-of-the-moment emotion when he put me on the Short List. Please tell him how much I appreciate it, but you now know what I already knew, which is that I am in no way qualified to be vice-president of the United States of America. I am not a student of national and international issues the way I should be. Please tell the senator that I will always be grateful for his letting me have this brief time in the limelight. But I will go quietly, and that will be that."

I extended my right hand across the table to Mr. McKinney to seal the gratitude and the deal. He took my hand in both of his, the way Jed Berryhill and everyone else did.

"You do not understand this process, Mr. Lieutenant Governor," he said. "In the confidence of this small room, in the spirit of honesty and candidness that has marked this luncheon event thus far, let me say to you, sir, that a man without strong views of his own is exactly the kind of person the senator and the party want as a candidate for vice-president."

I did not understand. And he must have seen from my face that I did not understand. He continued:

"What could be worse than having a presidential candidate and a vice-presidential candidate at odds with each other? What could be worse than having a vice-presidential candidate who continually has to trim his own views or shade his own words in order to avoid such an appearance? What, then, would be the best way to avoid that happenstance? I think the answer becomes obvious: Select and nominate a candidate for vice-president who is markedly lacking in strong views on the key issues that are likely to emerge in the campaign. So when asked he can honestly say, as you said on several occasions here now, that he has no view, no position, or that his opinion is not fully formed. It would then not be duplicitous or difficult for such a candidate to say to the press and to others that Senator Griffin's views and positions, the presidential candidate's views and positions, are in fact his as well because he has just come to his own conclusions as a result of studying the senator's and finding them to be correct and substantial."

"It sounds to me like you're saying only dumb people make good vice-presidents," I said.

"No, no, it is nothing like that. It is a matter of purity. The senator is interested in someone who does not have too many encumbrances to become a true Griffin man. That is all. He is seeking somebody pure, somebody who remains open to other views, somebody who is not weighted down with a record of words and positions that would be constantly getting in the way of the dialogue on the campaign trail."

Sure.

I turned down a second cup of coffee. Too much coffee in the middle of the day kept me awake at night.

"Now, if I may," he said, "a purely political question: What is your opinion of Gerald Ford, our incumbent president and the Republican nominee for president?"

"I think he's terrific," I said. "I wish he was a Democrat, but other than that I like him."

"As you certainly know, it is often the duty of the vice-presidential candidate to bear a heavier part of the burden of explaining the shortcomings of the opponent," he said, without his usual smile. "Would it be impossible for you to overcome your fondness for Mr. Ford and deliver whatever message about his shortcomings needed to be delivered to the American people?"

"No, not really. But why beat up on Mr. Ford? He brought the country together after Watergate and all of that. Why can't Senator Griffin just talk about what he would do differently and better?"

"Of course, that would be the thrust of the campaign."

His next question was: "Do you know any of the columnists?"

"I know Boggs."

"Boggs?"

"Frank Boggs of *The Daily Oklahoman.*"

"I was thinking more of the Safire, Evans and Novak, Will, Art Minow, Anthony Lewis, Joe Kraft, Tom Wicker types."

Some of those names sounded familiar, but I certainly did not know any of them.

"Columnists like to adopt candidates as pets," said Mr. McKinney. "Are you available for an adoption? Minow might be the best one for you."

"I'm not sure I understand what that means, but I guess so."

He asked a few questions about my wife and children and how I had happened to become the lieutenant governor of Oklahoma. And we shook hands.

"I was most intrigued by your call for assistance on the mummy search," he said. "I think you certainly succeeded in capturing the nation's attention on that."

I smiled.

"Happy Trails," he said at the door of the small wine room.

"You a Roy Rogers fan?" I asked in utter amazement. "Happy Trails" had been Roy Rogers's radio and TV sign-off.

"He was always my favorite cowboy star," said Richardson McKinney.

"Mine, too."

I was tempted to tell him how in the 1950s I had appeared onstage with Roy, Dale Evans, Gabby Hayes and Trigger when they had been in Adabel, Oklahoma, making a movie. It was my appearance there that had helped spring me into politics and led me to where I was now.

But it was late, so I just shook his hand again and left. Of course, there was a good possibility he already knew that story and that was the reason he had said "Happy Trails" in the first place.

I was beginning to think just about anything was possible.

The same driver and Cadillac were waiting outside to drive me back to the Claremont. I never did figure out what the 1971 Meursault thing was all about.

I told Jackie all about the lunch. It made her furious.

"What that old fool is saying is that they want somebody carrying a hatchet who is a dodo to run for vice-president of the United States. That is what he said to you. I cannot imagine your sitting there and taking that. Who do they think they are? I've been watching all of this nonsense on television. Speech after speech by people nobody cares about, before thousands of people milling around not listening. What kind of idiotic thing is that? They are the stupid ones. You are not stupid. Just because you do not know everything about arms this and economics that does not mean you are an empty-headed idiot. That is what they want. That is what they think you are. I am insulted for you."

"He also made me eat some kind of fish called grouper."

"Now that really is outrageous. As your wife, as an Oklahoman, as an American, I am up in arms. It is despicable. It is a disgrace. Not only do they call you stupid, they make you eat fish."

"I promised not to tell anybody what was said. I can't even write it up in my memoirs."

She started laughing and so did I. This whole thing was absolutely nuts. David Brinkley, what have you done?

Then a bellman in a uniform delivered a stack of notes, messages and other things. He set them down on a table in the main sitting room. It was stunning. Reporters from just about every newspaper and magazine and radio and television program I had heard of wanted interviews. The notes were mostly from people who wanted jobs if I did end up as either the candidate for vice-president or eventually as vice-president. Most had résumés attached. People who would advise me on the environment, the economy, labor relations, housing, the Middle East. People who were prepared to be my press secretary, my private secretary, my appointments secretary, my administrative assistant, my cook, my driver, my historian.

Historian. There amidst the telegrams was one from Sandra Faye Parsons. It said:

> YOU DID IT. THANK YOU, THANK YOU, THANK YOU. WE HAVE
> BEEN SWAMPED WITH CALLS. THANK YOU, THANK YOU,
> THANK YOU. LOVE AND KISSES. SANDRA FAYE.

Unfortunately, Jackie, as amazed as I was over all of the mail, notes and messages, was also reading the stuff. She also read that telegram.

" 'Love and kisses, Sandra Faye,' " she said. "Sounds like everything is suddenly available to The One-Eyed Mack."

"That's actually for real. She's the director of the Museum of the Cherokee Strip in Enid," I said. "She's the one who told me about the mummy."

Jackie, who in all things including jealousy was open and to the point, said: "Do all state employees sign off messages to their lieutenant governor 'Love and kisses'? By 'it' I assume she means making that dreadful pitch for Americans to check their attics and basements for a mummy? What is going on here, Mack?"

"Nothing," I said truthfully. "Nothing at all."

"What does this Sandra Faye look like?"

"Some people would probably think it would be accurate to say that she's ugly," I lied.

"How old is she?"

"Late sixties, probably," I lied.

David Brinkley, what have you done?

8
· · ·
GOD BLESS AMERICA

Art Minow's note said he was down in the lobby and would love to meet me for a few minutes. Could he come up, or could I come down? Mr. McKinney had gotten right on the job of arranging for a possible adoption.

Art Minow. I had read maybe two columns by him in my life. I could not recall if he was a liberal or a conservative, or anything else about him except that he played every year in some kind of important celebrity tennis tournament, and had written a book and talked on talk shows about how all politics, all government, all life could be seen as a game of tennis. I never paid any attention to what he said or what he meant by it. In Oklahoma it was the football coaches who talked that way. Look upon life as being a hundred yards long and the object is to get from here to there with the ball in your hand, was the kind of thing they said.

Jackie urged me to talk to Minow.

"I'll sit here with you," she said. "I've always wanted to watch something like this."

"Like what?"

"I don't know. That's why I want to watch."

Art Minow was thin, short, slick, dark, sixty. He came into the room and greeted both Jackie and me with great warmth and courtesy. I offered him a seat on the couch as Jackie and I sat down in chairs opposite. He was cool and smart enough to say or even imply nothing about Jackie's sitting right there with us. He acted like it was perfectly natural for the spouse to be present for an interview.

He pulled a small notebook out of his pocket. It was the kind stenographers use. He held it up and said, "How do we play this? My serve with notes on the record, or your serve with no notes off the record?"

I looked over at Jackie. She was smiling. But I could not read anything from that. So I said, "Let's make it off the record. Not even for our memoirs."

He smiled and put his notebook back in his pocket. "Fine with me, sir. Advantage yours." He took a short breath and said: "Can you Democrats really take Ford? Can you really? The Nixon pardon is there caught in the net, but he'll get points for that in some quarters for having put Watergate behind us. Does this country really need to have a president of the United States in the dock? Come on, please. Okay, so he is not the brightest guy in the world. So who says the president has to be the brightest guy in the world? He went to Yale for law school. He wrote a book about serving on the Warren Commission. The man can volley. He served in the House of Representatives for twenty years. He knows the issues, he knows the people. He knows who to call. Do you know that ninety percent of being president is knowing who to call and then calling them? Is it in or is it out? Jerry Ford can do that. So what do you go after him about? Griffin's not getting any free grandstand seats, that's for sure. Not by a long shot. The man's too liberal for the country. Much, much too liberal. Is the United States of America ready for a president from New Jersey? I say no. I say America will say no. So he's cleaned up toxic waste dumps with the Griffin Superfund Law. That's no six–love. Have you ever met anybody who committed murder or held up a 7-Eleven or cast a vote because of a toxic waste dump? I'll bet you haven't. Griffin's quirky. I mean quirky. That tomato-cream-soup-for-breakfast routine. If we know about that, there is no telling what else there is to find deep down in his ball bag. Maybe he ties up little girls in blue ribbons and plays doubles in the nude. Who knows? I do know and you should know that everything that man has done is going to get the going-over on the court, for the whole world to see like nothing has ever been seen before. Watergate has removed the grass court under which all can be swept. Nobody in my line of work wants it to be said that he let a crook or a quirky nut through the net into the White House, into the most powerful job on earth. Now you should know all of this, and I am sure you do. Good speech you made. Six–love. The mummy thing worked, six–love. I understand you are fresh on the issues, blank score on most everything, nothing really firmed up on many of the big ones. I guess that could be helpful if you can stay away from the ace. Who knows how the grandstand is going to read that? People don't always read things the way they are supposed to. I can tell you about that. I wrote a column once about gun control. I was trying to say that the people who argue for a national gun registration law had better look at their history, or something like that. I meant it as a caution against rushing into some drastic new legislation, and it was seen by some as an endorsement of gun control.

"What do you think your chances are of getting picked, of being the number-one seed? I see the odds against you. I really do. Dickson would help him. Florida, so there's the South. Armed Services Committee, so that helps fight off the peacenik image. But he's not even on the Short List. Manning is. Now there's trouble. Okay, he's from California and Griffin needs some geographic balance. But Manning? My God, he's almost as liberal as Griffin. And his wife's cuckoo. Into herbal cures for cancer and wrinkle removal. Speaking of wives, it's good your man Hayman's out of there. I heard about that wife of his. Got some kind of Kate Smith complex, is that right? No way a candidate for vice-president can get elected with a crazy wife. Not anymore. Those days are over forever. Watergate ended that, too. Carter might be good. Again, South. But all he's ever done is field lobs as a governor. No bullet serves have come his way. No offense about governors and lieutenant governors. That grin of his and all of that softness. Forget him. He gave Griffin a scare in the primaries, but no way he's national ticket material. Lyman? Maybe. With a small *m*. I think he ran for president mainly to give a boost to his lecture fees after he dropped out. My agent suggested I do something like that. Announce for president and then withdraw in a few weeks. He said it could add five big ones to the fee. Lyman's also a lefty. Did you see the way he tore into the CIA during the Church hearings? People remember that kind of thing. Who wants somebody one heartbeat away from the presidency who does not have the support and confidence of the CIA? That's the kind of question Griffin and McKinney had better start asking themselves before it is too late. Way too late. So that leaves you and Adair on the Short List. I'm putting my money on Adair. Moderate conservative, power serve. Chicago. World War Two hero, wife who only jogs and smiles. I give you only a very long shot, probably not even in the finals. Nothing personal. Just speaking as one professional to another. But wait a minute here, I have just been rambling on. I came to find out about you. McKinney said there was a lot of moxie behind that eyepatch and simple-country-boy serve of yours. I know the problem. I was raised on a farm outside Sioux City, Iowa, where people are told to speak only when spoken to and are taught all of the principles of hard work. Nobody thought I would amount to much. But that helps, actually. The best thing to be is underesti- mated. These politicians make the mistake of cozying up to people like me with their talk about how bright and electable and with it they are. We buy it, blow them up like balloons and then wait awhile and stick pins in the balloons and start all over again with somebody else. Better not to be a balloon in the first place. Keep the expectations low, keep the head low, keep the pinpricks away. If you'll pardon the expression, ma'am. Now, let's hear about you."

"I'm in favor of strict gun control laws," I said.

"I'm not," Art Minow said. "It's using the backhand when the forehand is needed. I thought there were a lot of hunters in Oklahoma."

"There are, but they're not stupid," I replied.

"That was a good mummy yarn," he said. "Be careful or it'll be all you'll be remembered for: Who was that one-eyed guy from Oklahoma who talked about the mummy? No offense on the eye. My father had two toes missing on his left foot. Somebody ran over them with a tractor when he was a kid. It kept him from ever developing a really top-notch serve, although tennis wasn't very big out in Iowa in his time, anyhow."

He looked at his watch, shook his head and stood. "I have

to be down at the World Trade Center in Wall Street in twenty minutes. With the traffic in this town, if I left an hour ago it could be tomorrow by the time I got there."

"Have another interview?" I said.

"Oh, no. Making a little speech to some broker types. I scheduled it to jibe with the convention. They're taking care of travel and hotel, plus a fee. I cover the convention at the same time, and all is six–love."

He shook Jackie's and my respective right hands and went to the door. "I always start off with a couple of jokes. Do either of you happen to have any new ones? Something about politics, the campaign, the Democrats?"

Jackie and I shook our heads.

He said: "Well, I'll go with the tried-and-true. Something about Jerry Ford not being able to chew gum and be president at the same time, or Ronald Reagan dying his hair orange, or Hubert being a textual deviate. They always get laughs. Do you know how many Teddy Kennedy dolls it takes to screw in a light bulb? Neither does he. Sorry, ma'am. Well. How many Teamsters does it take to screw in a light bulb? Twelve. You got a problem with that, buddy? I'm glad we could get to know each other."

And he disappeared out the door.

Jackie and I were left standing in the middle of the room staring at each other.

"I don't think I got adopted," I said.

Jackie nodded in delighted agreement. "Look at the bright side," she said. "We just heard for free what those poor stock market people are going to pay thousands of dollars to hear. And that, my dear Mack, is a real six–love."

Then we got ourselves together to go to the hospital.

• • •

The stack of messages had one from Cal that said he was taking his DC-9 and flying back to Oklahoma to "get lost." Cal also said that Joe's feelings were now hurt since I had not come to see him and it might cause him to have a relapse if I didn't get over to the hospital.

There was no limo anymore, so Jackie and I took one of those yellow taxicabs instead. The ride was a terribly frightening experience, the kind they used to put in Saturday-afternoon movie serials. The driver was a madman. I mean a real madman, the kind who in Oklahoma got taken away with force by court order to the state hospital in Norman. He cut in front of other cars. Drove at a speed that was more fitting on an interstate. Honked his horn continually. Tailgated continuously. And generally violated every rule of safety and courteous driving known to man. All in fifteen blocks from the hotel to the hospital. Jackie and I held each other's hands like the end was here. I imagined the awfulness of dying this way. In a yellow taxi in New York. Before finding out the ending to the Short List.

The taxi driver was dark-skinned, but other than that I could not tell a thing about him. He never looked back at us. He never said a word to us. He sat in the front seat behind a wall of glass and steel that was there to protect him from his passengers. There was a little metal tray kind of thing for sticking the money through to pay him. There was music playing loudly on the radio. Foreign kind of music that I imagined women in veils dancing and swirling their bottoms around to.

When we got out of the taxi, Jackie and I felt we were lucky to have survived.

I went to Joe's room by myself. Jackie went to the waiting room. She said it would give her a chance to call her office back in Oklahoma City. JackieMarts was having a problem with cereal sales.

As I approached Joe's room, I saw a group of people in white-and-green outfits standing together outside a room. They looked to be nurses, interns, orderlies, janitors, cleaning women. I heard someone singing. Kate Smith? No, it was Jill Hayman!

"From the mountains, to the prairies, To the oceans white with foam, God bless America..."

I arrived in front of Joe's room door and stood with the others.

"...my home sweet home! God bless America, my home sweet home!"

A young woman in white, a nurse obviously, whispered to me, "The governor asked if it was all right if his wife sang to him. We said sure. She is something, isn't she? Almost professional, if you ask me. She sounds like Barbra Streisand a little bit, doesn't she? She just stood up in there and sang. Without a piano or anything."

I joined with the nurse and the others in clapping.

The door opened. Jill Hayman was standing there, all big and Kate Smith–like in a smocklike yellow dress that fell from wide padded shoulders straight down all around her like a tent. She gave a kind of quarter-curtsy and smiled at the audience. The smile disappeared when she saw me. She beckoned for me to come to her, as the hospital personnel went away and back to their various duties.

"I was opposed to you coming, but he insisted," she said to me in a firm, nasty whisper. "Try not to make it worse for him than you already have. Remember, when you laugh, he cries. You cough, he throws up. You have everything, he has nothing."

God Bless America to you, too, Jill.

She moved out of the way and followed the hospital people down the hall.

Joe was in bed in a white gown. There was a copy of the *Enid News* on the bed beside him.

"How did you get a *News* way up here in New York?" I said as I walked in.

"It's two days old," he said. "Hi, Mack. I wondered where you'd gotten off to. I wondered if you had forgotten your old friend and governor. I wondered if you had decided to take over all my jobs and leave me here in this hospital to rot. I have been wondering about you, Mack. Did you hear Jill singing just now? She's a nightingale. She's a real nightingale. I hate it that she didn't get to sing at the convention. I really hate it. But at least she can say she sang in New York City. She certainly can. Who has to know it was in a hospital room? Who has to ever know, Mack?"

"Nobody, Joe. Absolutely nobody. I'm sorry I haven't seen you, but they didn't want you to have a lot of visitors at first."

He motioned for me to have a seat. I sat down in a hard-backed chair by the foot of his bed. It was a regular hospital room. A TV set came out from the wall on a rack. A table on rollers held a plastic pitcher of water and a small box of Kleenex. Pinned to Joe's bed, near his pillow, was one of those buttons at the end of a cord for calling a nurse. His head was attached to a machine by a couple of wires. His face was drawn and much whiter than usual, and his voice was much quieter. But other than that he seemed healthy and normal.

"You did a good job on the speech, Mack," he said. "Where did you get that mummy stuff? It wasn't in my speech."

"I know. I just stuck it in. Somebody at the historical society mentioned it to me."

"It's all these crazy people on TV are talking about. The one-eyed Oklahoman who put out a call for a mummy. It's crazy, Mack. All of this is crazy. But like I said, you did great on the speech."

"Not as good as you would have, Joe. Not as good as you."

"We'll never know, will we? We'll never know. Brinkley said they ought to run you for vice-president. What do you think of that?"

"Nothing much, frankly. Nothing much at all. When the time comes for Oklahoma to have somebody on the national ticket, you will be the one. Not me. Not some one-eyed guy who talks about mummies."

"Are you on the Short List?"

"I think so. But it doesn't mean anything."

"Either you are on the Short List or you aren't. If you are, it means something for you and for Oklahoma. I heard Griffin's man Vickers sits down with everybody on the List and asks him if they are queers or crooks. Then Richardson McKinney gives them the real going-over. Have they done that to you yet?"

"I just came from both."

"Have you talked to Griffin?"

"This morning, for a while. Yes."

"So you really are on the List." Joe moved his head around in a circle two times, like he was trying to fit his neck inside a tight collar.

"What's Richardson McKinney like?"

"Impressive, Joe. He's impressive."

"I knew he would be. I really knew he would be. Did he ask you about the multihead missiles? I heard he asks all of them about the multihead missiles. I had read up on them in *U.S. News and World Report*. I was all set to say 'MIRV' just like I knew what I was talking about. The doctors say I'll be able to fly home tomorrow. Good luck, Mack. Good luck."

"Thanks, Joe. I wish I knew what more to say."

"How about some advice from Buffalo Joe?" he said softly. "Do you want some advice from Buffalo Joe? Do you, Mack?"

"You bet," I said. "I have always treasured your advice on politics, Joe."

"You are an accident, Mack. An accident. Something happened to me and there you were. In politics that is all there is. Accidents. Politics is accidents. Accidents is politics. Tom decides to run, Dick doesn't, Harry wins because Tom's caught stealing. The next time, Harry loses because Tom drops out and Dick doesn't. Some crazy shoots Kennedy, Johnson's president. Muskie cries, Nixon's president. Eagleton has a shock treatment, McGovern's gone. Accidents, accidents. You are an accident. Never forget that. God didn't choose you, Jesus didn't choose you, the devil didn't choose you, the People didn't choose you, nobody chose you. Nobody chose any of us to do anything. We're accidents. I am the governor, you are the lieutenant governor. You are on the Short List, I am not on the Short List. You have one eye, I have two eyes. You knew about a missing mummy, I didn't know about a missing mummy."

He suddenly stopped talking and looked away from me. So I left.

Jackie waited until we were in a taxi on the way back to the hotel before dropping her awful news. Her secretary back in Oklahoma City said that our afternoon paper, the *Oklahoma City Times*, had a three-column photograph of me on its front page.

It was one of me in that Marine battle getup with Gunny Upchurch and the others at Iwo—Oklahoma's First Participatory War Game Facility. Right below it was an interview with Gunny in which he said that I had lost my left eye in the Korean War and that he and other veterans were proud of what I had done for veterans in Oklahoma and everywhere in America at that convention in New York City.

I told Jackie the story of my time at Iwo, which I had not told her before.

"My poor sweet Mack," she said when I had finished. She grabbed my left hand and squeezed it tight.

The taxi ride back was just as bad as the one coming over. But this time we barely noticed.

Back in our hotel suite, I first spent twenty minutes on the phone with the managing editor and various reporters of the *Oklahoma City Times*. I told them the truth of how I had lost my left eye, which never had been a secret to anyone in Oklahoma who wanted to know. I convinced them that I had never, ever claimed to have lost it in war. Any war. I said Gunny Upchurch had simply misunderstood. They agreed to run a corrective story the next day, also on the front page, and to tell the Associated Press and United Press International.

But it was already too late. I hadn't been off the phone in the sitting room five minutes when Jackie screamed at me to come into the bedroom. I raced in to see her sitting upright in bed staring at the television set. Senator Daniel Michael Griffin was talking to a reporter on the sidewalk in front of his hotel.

"He just called your name, Mack!" Jackie screamed. "He just confirmed he had put you on the Short List!"

The reporter, a TV correspondent who looked familiar but whose name I could not remember, now asked: "Is he qualified to be vice-president of the United States?"

"Yes, Annie, he is. That is why I put him on the List."

Another reporter asked how a man who had been only a county commissioner and lieutenant governor in Oklahoma could be ready to be one heartbeat away from being the leader of the free world.

Griffin said there had been examples in our history of people with long résumés of national government service turning out to be less than exemplary vice-presidents and even presidents. "So who can tell, Ben? Judgment is the real test. I think this man has judgment."

"How well do you know him?"

"Well enough, Phil."

"What do you think about the way he changed his name to something called The One-Eyed Mack? What kind of judgment is that a sign of?"

"I am an equal opportunity employer, Donnie. I do not discriminate against one-eyed people who decide to call themselves Mack."

Griffin was clearly uncomfortable, miserable. He kept trying to walk away. But the reporters, all of whom he clearly knew by their first names, wouldn't move out of his way.

Another said: "There's a story in an Oklahoma City paper today that says he claims he lost his eye in combat in the Korean War. Is that true? Is he a disabled veteran?"

A huge smile came across Griffin's face. "Mark, he lost that eye when he was a tad while he was watching some kind of exotic game called kick-the-can. It's quite a game. You take a tin can and place it on the ground in some central outside location. Someone is designated It. His competitors—

I believe any number can play—then run off and hide during a count of ten. . . . If you are fully fascinated, I can go on. . . . "

"Why is he claiming to have lost it in combat? Is he a liar, or what is he?"

The smile disappeared and Griffin said, "All I know about it, Carl, is what I just said. Now, please, I am late for an appointment. . . . "

"Have you heard about the five cars?" somebody yelled as he walked away.

The senator stopped and turned back. "What did you say, Mike?"

"AP has a story that a convicted-felon oilman gave the lieutenant governor five cars as a present. They were delivered to his house in Oklahoma City this morning. . . . "

"Mike, that is news to me," said Senator Daniel Michael Griffin of New Jersey. "I must run."

He stepped into a limousine, and a commercial for a hair-spray came on the television screen.

9

. . .

BUS SEX

I had closed the door to the bedroom, where I left Jackie reading over some weekly sales reports from JackieMarts. Vickers had insisted on seeing me in private.

Griffin's man John Vickers, The Walrus, of course did not say hello or anything like that to me. He just rolled in and went directly to a couch like he owned it and me. I assumed he had come about the five Ford Fairlanes. I was wrong.

He said:

"We have had a call from a newspaper in a place in Texas called Galveston. They say they have a story from a woman who saw you on the *Today* show this morning. She says she is a retired prostitute and that you were one of her customers."

"That is a lie. An absolute, one-hundred-percent lie. I have never traded with a prostitute."

"She said she had a sexual experience with you on a bus going to Beaumont, Texas, in 1949."

Oh my God!

"Is it true?" Vickers said, after a few beats of silence.

"Yes," I said. "But I was just nineteen years old. She sat down next to me and . . . well, you know, started playing around. When it was over she demanded three dollars. So I paid her."

"What was over?"

"The experience."

"You screwed this woman on a bus? Is that the story?"

"She brought me to a climax on a bus. You know . . . with her hand."

Now Vickers was silent for a few counts.

"Well, what do we say about this? We can confirm you paid a prostitute three dollars to give you a hand job on a bus when you were nineteen years old, or we can deny the whole thing."

"How can I deny it?"

"Were there any witnesses to this experience? Did you do it up in the front of the bus for all the passengers to see?"

"No."

"Okay, then. She's a dirty, immoral hag prostitute, you're the clean, moral lieutenant governor of Oklahoma. It's your word against hers."

"Why would any newspaper run such a story?"

"That's the business they're in."

"I don't think that is what John Hancock had in mind."

"We will tell them we could not reach you for comment. But eventually you're going to have to say something. Deny or confirm. The decision's yours. I strongly recommend you deny. Is there anything else you haven't told me?"

"Yes, as a matter of fact there is. I had a wet dream about Lana Turner at the Chanute, Kansas, YMCA summer camp when I was fourteen years old. But don't worry. The counselor told me Roy Rogers and General Eisenhower also had wet dreams."

Vickers pulled himself to his feet. "This is serious business, Mr. Lieutenant Governor."

"That I do not have to be told."

He shuffled his walrus self toward the door. "What *is* the deal on the five 1957 Ford Fairlanes?" he said.

"I'm going to return them. It was all a terrible, stupid mistake."

"Stay close in case something else comes up?"

"Yes, sir. Yes, sir."

"This really is serious business," he mumbled, as he tumbled himself out the door.

Jackie was still sitting on the bed with her JackieMarts sales reports. She was frowning and shaking her head.

"We're not selling cold cereal anymore, Mack. None of the stores is selling it. Cornflakes are down. So are the new healthy things and even the sugar stuff. I do not get it. Cold cereals are a natural for us. They have always been a good seller. What do you think happened?"

I sat down on the edge of the bed and said, "I have not the slightest idea."

Still looking only at her reports, she said, "You are on the Democrats' vice-presidential Short List. You are supposed to know everything. If the people of this country find out that you do not know ... "

"It may not matter, because I really may not be on the List much longer."

She put down her reports. "What's happened now?"

"There is something in my early life that I have not told you," I said. My voice and tone were as somber and serious as I could make them.

She grabbed my hands and pulled me right to her. "Tell me, Mack. Was it murder? You look like it was murder. Who did you kill? Was it self-defense? Did you use poison or your two hands? Have you been keeping the body as a mummy in the attic?"

"It was sex."

I felt her grip on my hands lighten ever so slightly.

"You mean you had a sexual relationship with someone else before me?"

"That's right."

"How long did it last?"

"About ninety seconds."

She dropped my hands. "I don't think I need to hear the details, thank you."

"The woman recognized me on television this morning and has gone to the newspapers. There's going to be a story."

She had gone rock-candy cold on me. "So why is it news that a man on the Short List had sex with a woman other than his wife before he was married?"

"She is a prostitute, or was at the time."

"A prostitute! Mack, no! You might have gotten a disease! Or shot! You idiot! Don't tell me a thing more!"

"It wasn't like that."

So I told her the whole story of Lillian the Come Lady, the story I had never told a soul and had figured I never would. I told her how I had gotten on the Texas Red Rocket Bus Company's Beaumont Limited in Galveston. How this side of High Island a woman in a bluish-purple dress had come back where I was and sat down next to me. How after a while she had put her hand on my leg. How in a few minutes I had come in my pants. How she had demanded three dollars on the grounds that that was the going rate for this kind of service in Galveston, where she worked. How she had threatened to tell the bus driver I had attacked her if I didn't pay up. How she had suggested the driver was her husband. How I had paid her three dollars. How I had had trouble drying off myself and my pants before arriving in Beaumont.

About halfway through the story Jackie grinned slightly. Then she smiled. Two-thirds of the way, she was in stitches. By the time I was through, she was in hysterics. "Mack, Mack, I love it. I just love it. You are wonderful." She hugged me and tickled me and got me laughing. "Mack, The One-Eyed Sinner. Here he is. Paid three dollars to a woman on a bus. Came in his pants and now he's through. Gone, gone from the Short List is The One-Eyed Mack. Gone, gone with come in his pants."

When we calmed down, I still had a problem. What should I say about it publicly?

I told Jackie the choices were not great. I confirm it and then live with headlines like: ONE-EYED VEEP SHORT-LISTER AD-MITS COMING IN PANTS ON BUS. Or I lie and then live with the fear that I will be proved a liar. ONE-EYED VEEP SHORT-LISTER LIED ABOUT COMING IN PANTS ON BUS.

Jackie, who had laughed so hard she brought up tears, wiped her nose with a Kleenex. Then she put her hand on my leg right up against the crotch like Lillian the Come Lady had.

She said: "Jackie the Drive-Thru Grocery Lady says deny it. By all means deny it. You must deny it. The American people will never elect somebody vice-president who is stupid enough to admit publicly that he did what you did on that bus. You have no choice but to lie. In the interest of America, lie. In your own interest, lie. In my interest, lie."

"Your interest?"

"I'm not sure I want the world to know I married a man who would be stupid enough to admit having done such a thing."

Oh, David Brinkley, David Brinkley, now what?

"Now you climb in this bed and take a nap," Jackie said. "This being on the Short List is wearing you out."

I was sitting in my underwear in the back of an open dump truck with Jackie, Lillian the Come Lady, Sandra Faye Parsons and David E. George, alias John Wilkes Booth. A dozen policemen on tricycles circled the truck and brought it to a braking, screaming halt. I stood and peered over the side. An officer who looked like my dad came over to me. It *was* my dad.

"President Griffin is dead. The Arkansas National Guard had him killed. Would you please raise your right hand, son?" said Dad.

I raised my right hand.

"Do you solemnly swear to uphold the Constitution of the United States?"

"I do," I said.

"Under the authority vested in me by David Brinkley, as a state highway patrolman of the State of Kansas, I hereby proclaim you president of the United States."

"Thanks, Dad."

Then I was sitting in my underwear in the back of a Flxible Clipper bus like the one Lillian the Come Lady and I had ridden from Galveston to Beaumont in 1949. Several men in dark blue suits, blue shirts with button-down collars, and dark red ties were standing at attention facing me. "Members of the Cabinet," I said, "I can no longer tolerate this hostility and abuse from the government thugs of Arkansas. I hereby

declare war on Arkansas for refusing to return our mummies.
I hereby order you to send the FBI, the CIA, the Marines,
the Bureau of Mines and U.S. Postal Service to invade Arkansas." One of the men said, "Sorry, President Mack, but
that is impossible. There no longer is a U.S. Postal Service.
It has been privatized into the Jackie Trailways Mail and
People Delivery Service, best known as JTMPDS."

I awoke with Jackie's mouth on mine.

"Wake up, Mr. One-Eyed Veep Short-Lister," she whispered.

Jackie had order me a tunafish sandwich and some fries
and a piece of apple pie for an early supper.

She also had another stack of messages and résumés that
had been brought up to the suite. "They're mostly from reporters and people like that," she said. "Except one from a
professor named Bearden. He said it was most urgent."

"That's some guy doing research on keynote speeches," I
said. "Nothing he has to say will ever be most urgent. Let's
go for a walk and think about what we do next."

The first sign that I was about to have one of the most
stunningly memorable experiences of my life came on the
elevator. After first staring at me for a few seconds, a middle-
aged blonde woman said, "You're that Mack, the mummy
man from Oklahoma, aren't you?"

"Yes, ma'am."

"I'm Miriam Wall from Rochester. That's in New York
north of here. Hang in there, Mack. You've got it. Don't let
'em run you off. Can I have your autograph?" She handed
me a piece of hotel stationery and ballpoint pen. I was still
writing "To Miriam Wall of Rochester with Sooner Greetings
from Mack," when the elevator door opened at the lobby
floor.

We stepped out. I finished writing, handed the paper back to Miriam Wall and looked up to a whole new world.

"There he is!" yelled a man with three cameras hanging around his neck. "Mr. Lieutenant Governor!" screamed somebody else holding a portable TV camera.

There was the noise of footsteps and movement. My way was suddenly blocked by a knot of people and television cameras.

More shouts.

"How many times have you had sex on buses?"

"What did that Blackwell get for giving you the cars?"

"The name? Why did you change your name?"

I smiled. I held up my right hand and shook it and my head no. I grabbed Jackie by her left elbow and tried to steer us around toward the hotel front door.

"Are you going to withdraw your name from the Short List?"

"Have you heard from Griffin?"

"Did Stan Musial really knock your eye out with a line drive?"

I stopped. Microphones of all sizes and types were shoved into my face.

"I have nothing to say about anything right now, except that I am honored and pleased that Senator Griffin is considering me along with several others for his choice to be the vice-presidential nominee of my party. As we say in Oklahoma, thank you for thinking of me. Now, if you please, my wife and I were on our way out for a walk. This is our first trip to New York City...."

There was a slight parting and I moved myself and Jackie toward daylight.

"Are you serious?" yelled a young brown-haired guy with only a notebook. "You've never been to New York before?"

"Dead serious," I replied. "Except when passing through once."

The reporter wrote in his notebook like I had just admitted to mass murder. ONE-EYED VEEP SHORT-LISTER ADMITS NEVER BEING IN NYC BEFORE!

Jackie and I broke away. I heard applause. The people behind the front desk, guests and bellhops were clapping for me! I waved to them all.

The doorman pushed people aside to let us in the revolving door. He saluted and said, "We're with you, Mack. Great speech. Good luck on the mummy."

Out on the sidewalk, a taxi driver leaning against his taxi yelled, "Yea, yea, if it ain't The One-Eyed Mack!" Two or three other drivers in line behind him jumped from their cabs. Somebody honked a horn. I waved. So did Jackie.

It was about six o'clock. Hot, still very light, and the sidewalk was jammed with people.

"Don't let the bastards get you down!" said a young man in a wrinkled light brown suit.

Two elderly ladies pushed evening newspapers in front of me and asked me to sign the story about me. I did, only glancing at the headline: KEYNOTER TOOK CARS, ACCUSED OF BUS SEX.

A jerky-looking guy in tennis shoes and a T-shirt with "I Love Wilkes-Barre" on it asked if he could take Jackie's and my picture with his Polaroid camera.

We came to a restaurant named The Superchief's, for Allie Reynolds. Allie Reynolds! The Superchief! One of baseball's all-time great pitchers and a native of Bethany, a town west of Oklahoma City. I looked inside. There was a gigantic oil painting of The Superchief in his windup, plus smaller photographs of him checking the runner at first, swinging a bat and doing things like that. Before we moved on, a man came out of the restaurant.

"You're The One-Eyed Mack, aren't you?" he said.

"Yes, sir."

"I'm The Superchief. Come in and have a cold one on me. Is this the missus?" It really was Allie Reynolds. The grin and the dark skin and the black hair.

I could not believe it was happening.

"I hear you made a great speech. I was out at the stadium and missed it. They're proud of you back in Oklahoma, I'll bet," said Allie. "How's the mummy thing going?"

People had gathered around us. Lots of people. I could feel their crush and breath.

I shook The Superchief's hand and said we had to move on. Thank you just the same for the invitation to have a cold one, I said. He handed me a small card with a colored picture of him in his New York Yankees pinstripe uniform. He said the restaurant normally charged for these things, but he wanted me to have one on him. I shook his hand again.

Jackie and I started moving again. Several people seemed to go right along there with us. One of the men who had been in the hotel lobby with a TV camera was now in front of us, walking backward so he could get shots of us from the front. I was sure he would trip if he didn't watch out.

We came to a huge hotel called the Plaza. I had heard of it. I remembered Walter Matthau was in a movie that took place there. He played three different characters in three different stories. We cut across an open space in front of the hotel, where a fountain was spewing out water. A young man and a young woman were wrapped in each other's arms and lying on the concrete at the base of the fountain. The woman's skirt was way, way up, and they were moving back and forth against each other like they were in a Jed Berryhill movie. I poked Jackie to look. She did. But as best as I could tell, nobody much else was looking.

Jackie spotted a store across the intersection that looked interesting. A toy store.

A young New York policeman whose long hair would not have been permitted on any Oklahoma police force stopped traffic so we could walk diagonally across the street to the store. "Don't give up, Mack," he said when we passed him. He also had a mustache like Groucho Marx's. That wouldn't have been allowed in Oklahoma, either. "We've got an all-points out on that Booth guy for you. Nothing yet."

The street was Fifth Avenue. *The* Fifth Avenue.

The toy store was called Schwarz, if I remember correctly. I had never seen a toy store like it. It had everything a kid could ever want. Up on the second floor there was even a great display of antique toys. My eye immediately went to a cast-iron bus about a foot long. It was an exact replica of a 1940s GMC Silversides, painted Greyhound blue and white. The only problem with it was the price. Seventy-five dollars. I could not imagine any sane person ever paying that much for an old toy.

The word had spread that we were inside the store. A group of twenty-five or thirty people was waiting for us when we came back out onto Fifth Avenue.

Several applauded. Many shook my hand. Some wanted autographs, or to have their pictures taken with us. They said things like, "We're behind you, Mack," "Give 'em hell, Mack," "Never quit, Mack." One man said he had done his pilot's training at Vance Air Force Base and he loved both

Enid and Oklahoma. A woman asked if I was related to a woman in Connecticut who had also lost her left eye.

Jackie and I did our best to look in the windows of the fancy jewelry, luggage and dress shops and bookstores as we walked down Fifth. The traffic on the one-way street was bumper to bumper. Eventually it stopped altogether. At least half of the cars as far as I could see back up the avenue were yellow taxis. Some horns started honking because of the traffic jam, I assumed at first. But they were for me. And the honking spread, and people rolled down their windows and yelled things at me. Nice things about staying on the List and not letting it all get me down and how great my speech had been.

"They're ganging up on you, Mack!" some man yelled. "Ignore 'em, Mack! F——— 'em, Mack." Back home he would have been arrested for yelling something like that on the street.

A young man rode up to the curb on a bicycle. "Everybody does it, Mack. Everybody." He then made an obscene kind of sign that I remembered from high school in Kansas that meant something close to masturbation. It was an obvious reference to the Lillian the Come Lady story.

Several people simply asked permission to touch me. An elderly lady with a dog walked up and said, "The *Times* says they're all crooks. All of them." I had no idea who she was talking about. One man from California said he was in New York for the Democratic Convention because he was a collector of political memorabilia. He wondered if I had anything on me that he could have. I said I was sorry that I didn't. He left me a cheap calling card with his name and address in case something turned up later. Two people asked me for money.

It was simply incredible. An astonishing, crazy experience.

The kind that happens mostly to movie stars. The kind that never happens to one-eyed Oklahomans.

Or frankly, to very many two-eyed Americans of any kind.

Jackie and I returned to the hotel ready to watch the second night of the Democratic Convention with my good friend David Brinkley.

There was more commotion when we walked back through the lobby of the Claremont, but most of the TV and other reporters were gone, so we made it fairly quickly to the elevator. There we were waylaid by Professor Cliff Bearden of Duluth Community College. He was wearing the same corduroy pants and checked sport coat.

"I have an emergency to discuss with you, Mr. Lieutenant Governor," he said. He had that same sincere look in his face. Only more so.

"Please," I said, "I have real emergencies to deal with right now. I told you we could get together after all of this is over."

He looked around to see if anyone could hear him. "I promise you, sir, that what I have to say . . . "

The elevator arrived, the door opened. I waved and stepped on it and away with Jackie.

"What was that all about?" Jackie said on the ride up. "He sure seemed exercised."

"All professors are like that," I said.

"No, they're not," she replied.

10
. . .
SORRY, DAVID

It was platform and old Democrats' night at the convention. Most of the platform things went through without too much of a fuss, except for planks on abortion and arms control. There were long, very long speeches from both sides on those and a few other topics but nothing worth remembering. The talks by George McGovern, Edmund Muskie, Hubert Humphrey, John Glenn, Morris Udall and some others were the same. With a gun to my head, I could not recall one thing any of them said. But that is hardly a headline. Being in politics, even in Oklahoma, often requires making and listening to speeches that must be made because of the politics of the moment but are not worth remembering. Even by the person who delivers them. Maybe Senator Griffin was right about speeches. It was all in the delivery.

Jackie and I opened Diet Pepsis and took chairs in the sitting room in front of the largest TV in the suite. It had a remote-control thing and Jackie wanted to switch around among the networks, but I insisted on loyalty to David Brinkley. It was David Brinkley's nod and few words that had started it all for me, so it would be NBC this evening and every other evening, no matter how it all turned out.

No matter how it all turned out.

It was strange watching something on television that was actually happening in the flesh twenty-five blocks away. It did not seem real or even possible that I had been on that podium in Madison Square Garden just twenty-four hours before. Not real, not possible.

But then during one of the abortion speeches, John Chancellor introduced a report from a correspondent I did not recognize about what he called "the vice-presidential sweepstakes."

There were shots of and words about all of us on the Short List. I was last. The correspondent said that by most accounts I remained on the List despite some "downer developments." As he went through them one by one there were pictures of Jackie and me on our walk by The Superchief's and down Fifth Avenue. It ended with the correspondent's saying: "Most observers I talked to say the story of The One-Eyed Mack may turn out to be the story of why only national politicians with well-investigated, well-scrutinized, well-tested and well-reported backgrounds normally make it to anybody's vice-presidential Short List. There are just too many risks involved in going with the unknown and uninvestigated, like this man from Oklahoma who calls himself The One-Eyed Mack. John?"

Chancellor turned to that extraordinary man named Brinkley. "What about that, David? What do you think of what is happening to the lieutenant governor of Oklahoma?"

David said:

"If you want to know what I think, I'll tell you. And it's this: The man comes up here, stands in beautifully for his fallen governor, gives the speech of the convention, impresses Griffin and most everyone else, and gets put on the Short List. Then along come the termites out from under the boards of his life. We, the press, overdo it, as is our tendency, and now twenty-four hours later we're talking about a man having a teenage sexual experience on a bus more than twenty years ago that just might disqualify him from being vice-president of the United States, a job, I think we must all remember, was described by John Nance Garner when he was vice-president as comparable to warm spit."

"Thank you, David," said Chancellor. "NBC's coverage of the Democratic National Convention will continue from Madison Square Garden in New York City in just a moment."

Thank you, David!

Unfortunately, NBC's coverage of the convention and thus of the vice-presidential sweepstakes did continue.

Toward the end, just after McGovern spoke, Chancellor came in with a news item. He said the Associated Press had just moved another story about The One-Eyed Mack, the lieutenant governor of Oklahoma. He said it had a Springfield, Missouri, dateline.

Springfield, Missouri? My back stiffened. My pulse stopped.

"The AP says a convict at the Missouri State Prison is claiming The One-Eyed Mack, as we now all call him, originally migrated to Oklahoma with his son—the convict's son—so one of them could be elected lieutenant governor and later pardon him—the father. The AP said the lieutenant governor could not be reached here in New York for comment. David?"

"That is just the kind of thing we were talking about earlier. It may, in fact, be true, but I doubt it. Any Tom, Dick, Harry or convict can now call a reporter and tell a story about this man from Oklahoma and get his name in the paper—and on television. It's a shameless way to treat a man who did no more than deliver a splendid speech."

"Thank you, David. We will be back in a moment."

Jackie and I had leaped to our feet in front of the television. Now we were frozen stiff, barely breathing.

That was because we knew what my friend David Brinkley did not.

The story from Springfield, Missouri, was in fact true.

Sorry, David.

The first thing I did the next morning was put in a call to Senator Griffin. It took a while, but he finally called me back. He could not have been nicer when I told him that I was going to have a news conference that day and what I planned to say. "Sorry about all of this flak, Mack," he said. "'Flak Mack.' That was an accident. I was not intending to pun about your misfortune." I told him I took no offense. We talked a few more seconds and suddenly Vickers the Walrus was on the line from another phone. And Griffin was gone.

Vickers said he would be glad to alert the press and make all of the arrangements for me to have a news conference at the Americana Hotel, where there was a big ballroom already wired and ready for such events.

"I will send over Maloney. Do you know who Maloney is? Probably not. He's a political consultant with a specialty. He's America's number-one hot potato on press conferences and interviews. He follows the Kennedy model."

I told Vickers that I did not need or want any such help, but he insisted and I said okay.

It wasn't long before Maloney arrived at my hotel suite door. Pete Maloney, age about thirty-two or so, was what Jed Berryhill would have been if he had been born twenty years later and had gone into political consulting instead of pornographic movie producing. Everything about him was overdone. His clothes were wrinkled and cheap, as if he had picked them up at a costume shop after having asked for something in wrinkled-and-cheap. Not only did his cornblond hair need cutting, it looked like it had been yanked and pulled to make it seem even longer. Not only did he talk, that was all he did. Continuously, uninterruptedly.

Here's what he said, standing in front of the picture window with his back to Central Park, much like Joe had done in his suite while rehearsing his speech.

"First, show up late. Six to eight minutes late. This will raise the anticipation level. Make these people think that you are in an important meeting, possibly going over some last-minute developments. It will make them restless. That's good. But don't be over eight minutes late. That gets them pissed. These people are like wounded banshees when they're pissed.

"Call each one by name. I know you won't know them going in. But ask all of them to identify themselves before asking a question. When they give their names, write them down on a little pad. And then when you give the answer say, 'Well, Bob, I am glad you asked about my murder conviction . . . blah-blah-boom.' 'Josephine, the answer to why I embezzled the money is . . . blah-blah-boom.' Why? Because you are dealing with the only group of people this side of Hollywood with bigger egos than politicians. They spend their whole lives trying to become important while saying they aren't. So when you call them by name, that says to every-one—their peers as well as their bosses back in the office—that they're important.

"Be self-deprecating. Knock yourself. Admit you're no Ein-stein, no Thomas Jefferson, no Franklin Roosevelt. Give them the 'I'm just a country boy from Oklahoma looking for a mummy' bit a time or two. But don't overdo it. You may be only the lieutenant governor of Oklahoma, but Senator Daniel Michael Griffin, David Brinkley and a lot of other people thought you were Short List material.

"Get hot at least once. I mean angry. Hit the podium or turn your face red. Say something like, 'I wish I could say what I would like to say, but I don't trust myself . . . blah-blah-boom.' Real humans get angry. These people are big about writing that somebody in politics is actually a real human. So get hot. You've been through hell the last twenty-four hours or so, remember. It would not hurt at all to have the stories say something like, 'An angry One-Eyed Mack denied . . . blah-blah-boom.'

"But do not cry. Even if someone walks in in the middle of the news conference and tells you your entire family and hometown have been wiped out in a terrorist attack, do not cry. These people's definition of a real human does not include crying. Only weak people cry. Weak people are not fit for public office . . . blah-blah-boom.

"Praise a question. Say how grateful you are it was asked. Say how delighted you are for the chance to set the record straight. Nobody will believe it except the reporter who asked it. But you can count on that one being vain enough to think you are just calling it the way you see it. If possible, pick a question from the *New York Times* person to praise. No re-porters think they ask better questions and deserve praise and attention more than people from the *Times*.

"If you get stuck for an answer and need time to think, tell a story. Any story. 'Hey, governor, is it true you also do it with prosties in the back of fire engines?' 'Good question, Roger, but I must tell you what my father said to me the day I graduated from high school. His name was also Roger, by the way. He and my mother met on a blind date at church. But back to my story. It was a rainy day. My dad, who delivered refrigerators for a living, because he had only an eighth-grade education, pulled me aside and said, Son, whatever you do with your life, be sure and do it with a grit and a grin . . . blah-blah-boom.'

"Try not to tell a lie, but if you have to, pre-label it so it can't come back to haunt you, so they can't say you didn't warn them it was a lie in the first place. Say something like, 'My memory may be faulty on that—so don't hold me to it or call me a liar later—but as I recall, I was in church having my new baby girl christened when the bank was robbed . . . blah-blah-boom.'

"Try not to be arrogant. These people hate arrogance in all people other than themselves. Remember above all else, as you look at them, that you are looking at people who for the most part have come to think of themselves as being more important than you and the rest of the people they cover.

"Try not to giggle. It's fine to smile and to laugh heartily, but not to giggle. These people have been known to destroy politicians for giggling.

"Any questions?"

I couldn't think of a one.

I had never seen so many These People. There were at least three hundred of them sitting in chairs, running cameras and tape recorders, or just wandering around. I knew that all of the stories about my problems had made me big news at a convention where there wasn't much else going on. I also assumed most now saw me as a weirdo hick freak, and they had come to hear and watch me confirm it.

ONE-EYED MUMMY-LOVING VEEP SHORT-LISTER ADMITS BUS SEX, PARDON SCHEME—SLOBBERS, PICKS NOSE!

I had had one brief experience with this kind of thing before. An incident involving false allegations about an Oklahoma-based Mafia group had brought several national reporters to our state. Joe had put me in charge of handling the problem, which I had done with C.'s help. I had even appeared at a press conference in a room outside Joe's office in the capital. It had been on the way out of that event, in fact, that I had said something that had come back to haunt me now. A reporter had asked me how I'd lost my left eye. The whole thing annoyed me, and before I knew it I'd told him Stan Musial had knocked it out with a line drive. Obviously some jerk didn't recognize Oklahoma sarcasm when he heard it, and now it had resurfaced somewhere among These People.

I was standing now in front of a podium on a stage in a ballroom at the Americana Hotel. It was that problem of how I had lost my left eye, in fact, that I spoke of first in my prepared statement.

I repeated the true story of watching the kick-the-can game. Then I told the Musial thing. Then I explained how Gunny Upchurch, owner and operator of Iwo—Oklahoma's First Participatory War Game Facility, had simply misunderstood what had happened. I apologized for any false impression anyone might have gotten about why my left eye socket was empty.

About my name. I explained how, after losing my eye, I had rechristened myself The One-Eyed Mack. Mack as in truck. I swore that I had had no intention to deceive anyone. I had just wanted to be known as The One-Eyed Mack, and it stuck. Now I was known by all in Oklahoma and elsewhere as Mack. My father, a retired captain in the Kansas State Highway Patrol, even called me Mack. No big deal, please.

I moved on to Cal Blackwell. Cal, I said, was an old friend of Governor Hayman's, who, yes, had been given a probated sentence for digging slanted wells to steal oil from his neighbors. Neither Joe nor I had had a thing to do with that. We knew him now as a stalwart Sooner citizen and supporter of the Democratic Party of Oklahoma. As far as the five 1957 Ford Fairlanes, I told the story of how Cal, on his own, as a surprise and without my knowledge, had had those cars delivered to my house. I assured These People that I had already made arrangements to return them, unopened and undriven.

And then, in keeping with the sports idea that a good offense is a good defense, I gave them something brand-new to chew on.

I said:

"I would also like to say that I accepted a Valium tablet from Cal on the afternoon of the Keynote Address. I did so in order to rest before accompanying Governor Hayman to Madison Square Garden. It was the first time I had ever used Valium. It had an effect and I was able to rest."

ONE-EYED VEEP SHORT-LISTER ADMITS ILLICIT DRUG USE!

That brought me to Lillian the Come Lady. Over Jackie's objections and persuasions, I decided to come clean on this story as well. I told the whole story, leaving out only a few of the more intimate details. Then I got my face red, raised my volume to a near shout and finished with this:

"I do not believe having such an experience when I was nineteen years old makes me some kind of unclean, immoral sex offender. I think it is a serious, unwarranted and outra-geous invasion of my privacy for the news media of this country to publish and broadcast such a story. I think everyone in this room and all other rooms where men and women of journalism gather should bow their heads in shame. The original publication was despicable, the repeat of it was des-picable, the silence about it is despicable. Only David Brinkley, as far as I know, has had the courage to speak out. The rest of you should rethink what you are doing in a profession that spreads stories like this. Don't tell me it is news, because it is not news. Don't tell me you had no choice, because we all have the power of choice. That is supposedly what distin-guishes us live humans from lost mummies and from the coyotes and skunks that run wild in the plains of western Oklahoma."

I looked up from the podium. The room was quiet except for the sound of cameras. The three hundred These People were silent. Some were writing things down. Others were looking away. Only a few looked directly at me. The TV lights made it difficult, but with my one eye I tried to gain eye contact with all of those who did.

I pounded my right fist on the podium and yelled: "I would particularly like to get my hands on the scum reporters who yelled questions like, 'How many times have you had bus sex?' You call that journalism. I call it gutterism. I will say no more because I do not trust myself to know where to stop."

"Questions!" somebody with a male voice yelled from the back of the room.

"Not yet," I said sternly. "Not yet."

I took one of the deepest breaths of my life, looked back down at my statement and quietly continued.

"Now, the story from Springfield, Missouri. That story is also true. It also happened more than twenty years ago. The man who made the statement last night is Henry Lester 'Big Bo' Bowen. He was the father of Tom Bell Pepper Bowen, my best friend, who died a Marine hero in Korea. Big Bo was a bank robber who was serving time at the federal penitentiary at Leavenworth when Pepper and I fell in together and became friends. We went by to see him one day, and Bo asked Pepper to go to Oklahoma to become lieutenant governor. He said he had twelve more years before he could get out of Leavenworth, but unless he was pardoned in Oklahoma, that would not mean freedom. That was because he was also due to serve time in Oklahoma for a grocery store robbery in Muskogee that went sour. Big Bo said Pepper then had twelve years to do what he had to do to become lieutenant governor of Oklahoma. He said it was better to go for lieutenant governor than governor, because, he had heard, it was much easier to get the job. So we went off to Oklahoma and settled in Adabel down in the southeastern part of the state. The Korean War was on and Pepper went off to the Marines. He threw himself on a hand grenade to save the lives of his comrades. He was blown to bits. He was honored posthumously for his heroism and valor above and beyond the call of duty that resulted in his making the ultimate sacrifice for his country.

"His widow, Jackie, and I later married. We are still married. I went into local politics in Oklahoma and eventually became lieutenant governor, a position I still hold. Did I run for lieutenant governor in order to fulfill the promise made to Pepper's daddy? No, I did not. It is a simple coincidence that I ended up lieutenant governor. Big Bo's statement last night in Springfield was the first I had heard from or about him in more than twenty years. The reason is that he apparently forgot a stint he owed the State of Missouri for a gas station robbery that somehow superseded the appointment he had at the Oklahoma State Penitentiary in McAlester. So he's still serving that. I would be less than honest if I did not confess that since becoming lieutenant governor I have occasionally dreaded the possibility that my phone might ring and Big Bo would be on the line. But as I say, it never happened. And that's the story of my involvement with Big Bo Bowen.

"I did have one more thing to say, but if there are some questions about what I have said so far, I'd be delighted to deal with them now."

"If he had called, would you have gotten him a pardon?" somebody yelled.

"Would you each please identify yourself and your organization?"

"Jay Hawkins, the *Times*."

"New York?"

There was some pleasant laughter and Hawkins said, "Yes."

"Great question, Jay," I said. "*The* question. I am delighted to answer it. I am delighted to be able to say, No, Jay, I would not have tried to get him a pardon."

There was another round of laughs.

I called on a woman in a blue dress.

"Marge Anderson, UPI. Do you think the planting of all of these stories about you was part of a conspiracy by one of your opponents for the vice-presidential nomination?"

"Do you, Marge?"

"Sorry, sir, but I ask the questions...."

"My answer is no, Marge," I said. "It's absurd to even suggest such a thing."

There was a question about the motives of all people who had come forward with stories about me. I said I had no idea, that maybe you—These People—could answer that better than I could. Somebody wanted to know how I thought all of this was playing back home in Oklahoma. I said only time would tell. I was asked for the tiny details of how those five Ford Fairlanes got in front of my house, and why Fairlanes, and was I sure I was not a financial partner of Cal Blackwell's?

And that was pretty much the way it went until the bomb went off. The bomb being Cliff Bearden, director of the Center for the Study of the Speech in American Political Life at Duluth Community College in Minnesota.

I saw him coming down from the back of the room while I was answering a question from Tom Ratchet of *The Boston Globe* about why I had chosen Stan Musial in my lie about losing my left eye.

"Stan the Man was my hero when I was a kid and St. Louis Cardinals fan in Kansas, Tom. He was simply the very best. The best . . . "

"I have a question! A serious question!"

It was Bearden. He had arrived right down front and was yelling up at me.

These People shouted at him. "Hey, sit down!" "Get him out of here!" "This is press only!" "How'd he get in here?" "Security!"

I then made one of the dumber moves of my life. I held up a hand for quiet. And I insisted that Bearden was fine and legitimate and that if he wished to ask a question, I certainly had no objection.

"That keynote speech you made was stolen," Bearden said. "Except for the opening and the mummy part, there are not five complete sentences in it from start to finish that are original. . . . "

There was a din from the reporters.

"Wait a minute," said I, Mr. Cool, Fair and Pleasant. "Are you making an accusation of plagiarism?"

"I am indeed." He held up his right hand and pointed the forefinger at me like a sword in a bad pirate movie. "I hereby accuse you of plagiarism! I hereby accuse you of plagiarism of a scope and extent never before seen in the world of American politics! I hereby charge that your speech was a pasteup from ten different keynote speeches of the past!"

I thought of pounding Cow Cowell's basketball head with a Louisville Slugger baseball bat autographed by Stan Musial.

Bearden lowered his sword and turned to the stunned These People. He held up a stack of papers. "I have in my hand the proof. Don't take my word for it. I have several extra copies. I have marked his speech and shown where every sentence came from. From the Democratic keynote address of Alben Barkley in 1948. From Earl Warren's to the Republican convention in 1944. And from other Republicans—Douglas MacArthur in '52, even Harold Stassen in '40—and other Democrats—Frank Clement in 1956, Congressman William Bankhead in 1940. The only really original lines are those at the top and the few sentences about the lost mummy."

Like dogs to raw hamburger, These People descended on Bearden. In a matter of minutes, all copies of his documents were gone. Those who did not get their own were angry. Those who had them refused to share. There was some pushing and pulling and shoving. For a few moments, I thought bedlam—a riot, even—was about to break out.

But then, like going from a football game to a funeral, things suddenly got serene and quiet. I was still standing at the podium. One of These People yelled:

"Mr. Lieutenant Governor. Larry Nielsen. The *Times*. The *Los Angeles Times*. Your reaction to this plagiarism thing?"

"Great question, Larry. I am delighted to have this opportunity to say I have no idea what this is all about."

"Peg McKinley, *Boston Globe*. Who did you think wrote the speech?"

"It was prepared for Governor Hayman by a writer in Oklahoma, Peg."

"Who? What writer?"

I said only, "You've never heard of him, Peg."

The reporters didn't wait for me to call on them anymore. They didn't remember to identify themselves. They just shouted things up there at me. I said nothing back, so after a while it all stopped and things got quiet again.

I said:

"I have nothing more to say about this speech thing or anything else. I would simply like to finish my prepared statement. As I said a while ago, I did have something else to say after the questions. And here it is:

"Earlier today, before coming to this event, I spoke to Senator Daniel Michael Griffin on the phone. I asked him to no longer consider me for his running mate, to please remove my name from the Short List. I told him the various reports about me and my background have become a distraction and would continue to be such if he did, in fact, select me and the convention officially nominated me to be the vice-presidential candidate of the Democratic Party. I told him how honored I was, for myself and for the people of Oklahoma, to have been placed on the Short List. And I wished him well in his campaign and said I looked forward to viewing the Griffin administration with pride from my enthusiastic supporting vantage point in the Sooner State of Oklahoma.

"And that, ladies and gentlemen, is it. I now plan to return to Oklahoma and resume my duties as lieutenant governor under the leadership of that fine son of Oklahoma, Governor Joe Hayman. Thank you for coming here this afternoon."

I gave Bearden, who was standing dumbstruck in front of me, a little wave and headed toward the side door. Maloney, America's hottest potato on press conferences and interviews, was standing by the door with one very big grin on his face.

Several of These People crushed around me, but I kept moving toward the door and Maloney.

"Do you see yourself as a victim?" one of the reporters yelled.

"No more so than I did that day Joe DiMaggio cut out my eye with his cleats sliding into third," I said, giving them a little something to remember me by.

Maloney helped me through the door. Two security men joined us in the hallway and guided us both toward the outside and a car Vickers had provided.

"What kind of marks would you give me?" I said to Maloney as we walked.

"A-plus. Kennedy-like. A–double plus. These People will remember this one for a long time. So will I."

So will I.

Then, out of nowhere as always, appeared the young man from *NightTalk with Rod Label*.

"Rod wants you tonight," he said, pointing at me again like he was Uncle Sam on the recruiting poster. "We'll send a car to your hotel at ten-thirty on the dot. Deal?"

I said nothing, moved nothing. He handed me another card with his name and a phone number on it. "Until then, good-bye," he said, and disappeared.

Out of another nowhere came a young woman who identifed herself as a representative of *NewsWeekly with Joanne Mayer*. "Joanne respectfully invites you to be her guest, on an exclusive basis of course. Please, she said. Please. She has the audience, sir. She really does. She is *it*, right? She really is."

I took her card.

Maloney followed me into the backseat of the car and told the driver to hold on a minute.

"Look," he said, "the rules for a television interview are different from the news conference bit. Okay?"

I told him that I had some good experience with that from being interview by Jim Hartz on *Today*.

"The Hartz way is the Nice Way and that is yesterday in the business. It's over, dead, deceased, green, decayed, buried, cremated, gone, blah-blah-boom. You'll never be treated like that again by anybody anywhere near a national TV camera.

"So. First thing is to decide before you get there what it is you came to say. One thing. Not two things, not three things. One thing. Say it to yourself, say it to yourself, and say it to yourself. Then no matter what is asked, that is what you say. They say, Why did you really pull out? There are rumors you were paid a million dollars by the Mafia blah-blah-boom. You say, I did it because I won the North Yemen lottery and who needs this kind of grief blah-blah-boom. What time is it, Mr. Lieutenant Governor? I know the time because I won the North Yemen lottery and who needs this kind of grief blah-blah-boom.

"Try to stay away from straight yeses or nos. These inter-viewers are sitting there with a million follow-ups. But if you never answer the first one directly, they'll go crazy trying to follow up. They'll have to listen to what you're saying, and they don't have time for that. Gives you a little advantage.

"No anecdotes. They are great at a news conference but

nowhere in a TV interview. They'll be in a commercial before you finish, and you'll have blown the deal.

"No heat. Anger works at a news conference but doesn't in TV interviews. They say, Is it true your wife is a prostie and your kids are on drugs and your father is a blah-blah-boom hermaphrodite? You smile and say, Maybe. Offer no explanation, just smile and say, Maybe. Or, Who knows? Or whatever. Never attack the interviewers. Never. It's their show. People tune in because they like the people who star on it. They don't know you. You attack their star, you are in trouble. No matter what, smile. No heat.

"Do you Oklahomans have any quaint expressions?"

"Like what?"

"Like 'smooth as the skin on a baby bear's testicles,' blah-blah-boom?"

"No."

"Make up one or two. Colorful, memorable. So no matter what you say, the people will come away saying, 'Did you hear what that guy said? "Running for vice-president is what we in Oklahoma call putting mayonnaise on mashed potatoes."' Blah-blah-boom."

Mayonnaise on mashed potatoes?

"It's like your mummy thing. No matter what, they remember that. Always they will remember that. Rod Label is a special case beyond what I just said. Want to dry-run it?"

I said nothing, so he said, "I'm Label, you're you. The first question is: Are you really quitting, or is this just a setup to make people plead with you to stay on the Short List?"

"No, I mean . . . "

"What is the real story about what happened on that bus?"

"I told the . . . "

"So you failed in your campaign to get the vice-presidential nomination?"

"I didn't camp—"

"Why would an honest man change his name?"

"I told the . . ."

"What are you hiding? Tell the American people now what it is you are so afraid of."

"I am not . . ."

"That's all our time for tonight. Thank you, Mr. Lieutenant Governor, for being with us. We'll be back with another person in the news to abuse, right after these seven straight commercials."

I shook my head and laughed. "You never let me finish a sentence," I said.

"Exactly, sir. Exactly. Hit and run. Now if it's Joanne Mayer . . ." Maloney tossed his head around like he had a head of long curly red hair, fluttered his eyes and reached over almost in my face. In a husky whisper he said, "Mr. Lieutenant Governor, would it be asking too much for you to describe exactly how you felt at the moment of climax on that bus in 1949? The story is in the details. From the beginning, oh, please. Blah-blah-boom."

Maloney sat back up and said, "Any questions?"

"Would you go on either of these programs if you were me right now?"

"No way. You're dead. You just ran your own funeral. Why let them run another one, blah-blah-boom?"

He stuck his right hand over at me. "I think we could have turned you into something really viable."

"Thank you."

Blah-blah-boom.

Jackie and I flew back to Oklahoma City that night on Braniff. Jackie said I deserved to fly home first-class. She said she could treat her ticket as a business expense for JackieMarts

189

because of all the work she had done for the company on the cold cereal problem.

We were relaxed and eating a cold-cuts snack with brown bread when she gave me what I expected to be the final news bulletin from life on the Short List.

"Hammerschmidt of Trailways called while you were having your press conference," she said quietly, like she was reporting on the growth of the Bermuda grass in our backyard. "He said he was sorry to say that he was not going to be able to pursue the big merger deal with JackieMarts after all. 'This publicity about your husband. It would not be good for the venture to be associated in the public mind with such activities.'"

"Did you ask what activities in particular?"

"I didn't, but I am sure he meant that incredibly sordid, dirty, perverted thing you paid that awful woman to do on that bus. Hammerschmidt said he felt sorry for me and the family and said if I needed anything to please call. Like we had had a death in the family. Mack, oh, Mack. How could you have done this to me and the children and Trailways?"

BUS SEX KILLS TRAILWAYS–JACKIEMART DEAL!

We laughed and Jackie put her hand on my leg right up against my crotch. I made a deal of slapping her hand away in a gesture of indignant shock.

It was a smooth, soothing, peaceful flight. And by the time we landed at Will Rogers Airport, I had convinced myself that the turbulence and excitement of the Short List would end when the 707's wheels touched me and them down on Sooner soil just before midnight.

Not quite.

11

. . .

NOT QUITE

There were a couple of hundred people with signs and a band with great Oklahoma music to greet Jackie and me when we got off the plane just before midnight. MACK, WE LOVE YOU and OUR HERO MACK, BOOMER MACK and GO FOR IT, MACK were among the messages on the signs. "Go for it, Mack"? The band, which was from the high school in Adabel, where we used to live, played "For He's a Jolly Good Fellow," "Boomer Sooner" and a medley of tunes from the musical *Oklahoma!* I was delighted to notice they omitted "Poor Jud (Is Daid)," the tale of a smelly guy who lies moldering in the grave.

The mayor of Oklahoma City, an old friend of mine named Johnny Potts, was there to shake my hand and hug Jackie. He presented me with a proclamation declaring the next day "Mack Our Veep Day" in the capital city.

C. was there in his black Lincoln command car to speed us from the airport to our home. It was pretty dark out on the tarmac, and lights from little portable TV cameras made it even harder to see. So it was only as we were about to get into his car that I saw Gunny Upchurch and the troops from Iwo. There were about a dozen of them, half U.S. Marines and half Japanese soldiers, all duded up in their outfits and dirty faces. They were standing at attention in a two-rank formation over by a fence. I said a terrible word to myself, drew a breath of patience and went over to them. I had to. All channels were watching.

Gunny smiled and extended his hand, which I took. "Welcome home, Conquering Hero Skipper Mack," he said.

"Thank you, Gunny," I replied.

"I hope you didn't mind my giving the paper that picture," he said.

"I hope you didn't mind my explaining there was a misunderstanding about the Korean veteran business."

He was still grinning as the cameras continued to record our right hands still shaking one another. "Not a bit, Skipper Mack. All the publicity has given our business a real M-1 sniper shot in the arm. I am forever in your debt."

I thanked him for coming, removed my right hand from his and returned to C.'s car.

C. did all of the talking on the way in.

"You really are some kind of hero right now, Mack," he said. "You're as big as Will Rogers and Jim Thorpe and Nita Pickens of Perkins Corner all rolled together. Every TV station in the state's been running huge hunks of that New York press conference of yours. My God, you gave them what for. People are talking about naming turnpikes and roadside parks for you. The *Daily Oklahoman* and the *Tulsa World* want you to go for governor. The mummy thing is the damnedest thing of all, Mack."

Then, to Jackie's annoyance—she never had felt the affection for C. that I did—he finished the story about the Pickled Pigs in Purcell. He said it turned out the pigs liked whiskey, at least the cheap bourbon they were being served. They got hooked. They got drunk and stayed drunk. The owner called the local sheriff, who arrested the other farmer. A JP who was a friend of both ordered the whiskey server not only to stop giving whiskey to the other's pigs but also to pay a fifty-dollar fine plus all rehabilitation expenses.

"Rehabilitation expenses?" I asked.

"Yes, sir. To get the pigs off the booze without causing them severe mental and physical problems that will make them not as good and worth as much at slaughter time. Can you imagine the stink there'd be if somebody took home a slab of bacon and discovered it was drunk? The sheriff told me the judge ordered him to find out if there was a kind of AA for pigs."

I laughed. So did C. And after a while so did Jackie.

It was good to be home.

I turned on the television in our bedroom as Jackie and I undressed, and sure enough, Brinkley and all the rest were still on the air, still talking about the Democratic National Convention still going on at Madison Square Garden. The big news was that Senator Griffin had selected Adair of Illinois as his running mate, just the way Art Minow had said he should.

Johnny Potts put together a parade through downtown Oklahoma City the next day at noon. Jackie and I rode in a great new red Chrysler convertible. The Adabel band led the way, and the Oklahoma County Sheriff's Mounted Posse, an old firetruck from the Oklahoma Firefighters Museum and a 1946 Flxible Clipper bus from the National Motor Coach Museum in Oklahoma City brought up the rear. Nobody but me knew it was on a Flxible Clipper of the same model and vintage that I had had my experience with Lillian the Come Lady. I marked it up as an interesting coincidence of inconsequential history that nobody else ever needed to know about. Not even Jackie.

It was a typically hot, bright Oklahoma July day, but hundreds of wonderful Oklahomans turned out on their lunch hour to wave and cheer and hold up signs. Again, several of them said things like GO FOR IT, MACK. Some of the people yelled similar or other warm and friendly things at me. It was strangely like our walk among the people of New York City. I expected The Superchief to come out of a restaurant and shake my hand again. The only things missing were the obscene gestures and the yellow taxis and the unhappiness.

The little parade ended up at the Park Plaza Hotel, Oklahoma City's finest. There we went inside to a really nice sitdown lunch of mock drumsticks and broccoli with members of the Oklahoma legislature, state officials and friends. Johnny Potts called me an Oklahoma hero bound for glory. I responded by saying if there was glory to be won from this it would be won in the name of Oklahoma, not in mine.

And I made a special point of praising Governor Joe Hayman for his courage in the face of physical adversity and expressing my hope that he would soon be back at his desk, at the helm of our beloved Sooner State.

That night we had a small family dinner at home. All four of our kids were there to hear chapter and verse about what had happened in New York City. Our son, Tommy Walt, said that while watching me deliver the keynote speech, he was the most nervous he had ever been in his life. Tommy Walt owned and operated T.W. Grease Collectors, Inc., the largest restaurant grease collection business in Oklahoma and the Southwest. He told me this dinner was not the place, but he did want to talk to me soon about a business thing that had come to his mind as a result of my time in the national sun. He said it was not urgent but it was important. I said I would drop by his office one day soon.

His twin, Walterene, who was a nurse in Tulsa, said she had watched the speech with some other nurses in the intensive care ward at the hospital where she worked. It was good she had watched it there, she said, because she was fit for oxygen and CPR by the time it was over. She wanted to know if I thought I might have been chosen for the ticket if all of that "stuff" hadn't come out. I told her it was unlikely. Jackie told her it was likely. I told her politics was accidents, accidents were politics. Our other two kids, Stephanie, seventeen, and Cathy, fifteen, wanted to know mostly about what the hotel was like and why I didn't get to meet Julie Christie, Jack Nicholson, Warren Beatty and some of the other movie stars they saw on TV at the convention.

I did a great number of television, radio and newspaper interviews that day and the next. All were done the Nice Way, so I had no call to use any of Maloney's rules and guidelines. The end results were prominently and profusely broadcast or printed throughout Oklahoma. There were stacks of telegrams and letters at the office and at home that had come from all over the country. Most were from people saying congratulations or some such, but there were also some from people who wanted something. Like the shirt and underwear I had worn the night I had made my speech. There were a few condemnations, particularly of the bad example

I had set for young people by buying illicit, grimy sex from a prostitute on a bus. But most of the requests were for my presence. People wanted me to make speeches for a fee or free, or to accept an award. Five colleges and universities offered honorary degrees in January, four lecture bureaus wanted me as their client, a nursing home chain and five savings and loans wanted me on their boards of directors.

It was a surprise, frankly, to find out how many people all across America were just waiting to pounce on the next guy who got a moment in the sun.

There was one person I did not want to see or talk to. Cow Cowell was his name.

I still had not squealed on Cow. I deflected all questions about who had actually constructed that keynote speech for Joe and me. I had decided without a lot of thought that I would handle Cow in my own way, in the due course of time. I was not a terribly vindictive man by nature, but I did believe that people should have to live with the consequences of their actions. Cow Baby deserved some kind of remembrance, some kind of token consequence of the dastardly act he had committed. It was like when I was seven years old and my dad spanked me several good ones with his Kansas State Highway Patrol leather holster belt for filling up all of my sister's underpants with mud. I had done it in retaliation for her having spit on the remaining three toll house cookies she did not think I deserved to eat. After Dad walloped me, he said, "I would be letting you down if I let you get away with this, son."

I would be letting you down if I let you get away with this, Cow Baby.

I thought of a lot of things. Like having him arrested on the pot charge, getting his old hardware store condemned, having his girlfriend's parents come and take their little girl home. I was surprised, in fact, at the childish awfulness of some of those other things that leaped briefly to mind. They ranged from anonymous phone calls and notes to some Watergate-type dirty tricks, like having 1,500 cheeseburgers with fried onions or a dozen newly born lion kittens delivered to him COD, Pauls Valley.

Nothing seemed exactly right, but I felt compelled to do something. I owed it to myself and to the greater good called justice to do something. I had not yet zeroed in on what that something would be, when I walked into my office one afternoon and there he was, sitting in a chair facing my desk. I did not shake his hand or say much more than hi. I just went around to my chair behind the desk and sat down.

I considered myself a gentle, nonviolent man. I had no use for guns and have never owned one. But sitting there looking at Cow Cowell, I very much longed to see what a small bullet hole would look like right between his two blue eyes right there in the center of his orange basketball face.

"What do you want?" I said.

"I want to know what your plans for me are," he said, his voice as full of itself as always.

"I am planning to have you shot between the eyes with a small-caliber pistol," I replied.

"Seriously."

"Seriously," I said, and then asked, "For the record, why did you do it?"

"You were pressuring me, threatening me with arrest. I had to do something. So I went to the library and did some special research. I figured nobody'd ever notice. Can you believe there's a guy up in Minnesota studying these kinds of speeches?"

"You should go to jail for this."

"For stealing words for a politician? Come on. If they did that, every politician in America would be in jail. It didn't hurt you that much, anyhow. You were already down the tubes because of the hand job on the bus. Hey, I must say that was a dazzler. I always had you figured for Mr. Buttoned-up Straight. You're the first politician I ever heard of who was into bus sex."

"I am not into bus sex!"

"Hey, no need to yell. I can understand why you're upset. I have come with an idea for how to make it all up to you. Seriously."

I said nothing. He kept talking.

"What would you think of my ghosting a book with you? *My Short Life on the Short List* by you as told to me. We'll split everything fifty-fifty. I know some publishers who'll jump at it. You won't have to do anything but talk into a tape recorder for a few hours. Tell everything that happened from the time you got to New York until the time you got back here. I'll take the thing, transcribe it, purple it into some prose, and we're at the bank."

I regretted very much my position on gun control. I regretted very much that I was a gentle, nonviolent person. I wanted very much to smile pleasantly and say, "Why, certainly, Mr. Moo. That is one terrific idea. You bet. Count me in. Have you got a tape recorder on you? I will begin immediately. Yes, sir." Then I would open my middle desk drawer and say, "But maybe we should sign some kind of paper between us so we will each know the arrangement." I would reach into the drawer as if going for pen and paper, but instead would emerge with a silencer-equipped small pistol in my hand. I would point the pistol at a spot right between his two blue eyes in the center of his orange basketball face and pull the trigger.

What I actually said was, "Get out of here before I call the capitol police to throw you out. I would not allow you to ghost something for me if you were the only ghost left on the face of the earth."

He stood up casually, in no hurry, like my words did not matter. "All right, then," he said. "No hard feelings."

"There will always be hard feelings," I said. "Always."

"That was a good bit about the mummy, by the way," he said. "I did not mind one bit your changing my speech that way. Well done."

"Out!"

"Are you going to tell about it, or aren't you?"

"Tell what?"

"You know. That I was the one who did the speech."

"I haven't decided."

"You've got me by the short hairs, Mr. Truck. Plagiarism works worse in my line of work than it does in yours. I'd never get another decent assignment from any magazine or whatever."

"Don't call me 'Mr. Truck,'" I replied.

It was thirty minutes or more after he was gone that I was struck by what having him "by the short hairs" really meant. It meant that every day forevermore he would wonder if this was going to be the day I had decided to tell the world what he had done.

It wasn't as happy a thought as the one about putting a bullet between his two blue eyes, but it helped.

Only thirty seconds or so after that thought it occurred to me I had a problem concerning Sandra Faye Parsons that was a lot like Cow's with me.

Someday I knew I would hear from her with a report on the search for the mummy of David E. George. Or we would run into each other in the course of our respective duties for the people of the State of Oklahoma. I could handle all of that if and when it happened. The problem, of course, was Jackie.

Of course.

What happens if and when Jackie ran into Sandra Faye Parsons at a luncheon, dinner or some other kind of function? Oh, my, Mack told me you were ugly and old instead of gorgeous and thirty-five. Oh, my. Or what if Jackie saw her picture in the newspaper or on television? Mack, dear, I thought you told me this historian was ugly and old. Why did you tell me that, Mack?

When we were in the hotel room in New York and I had told her about Lillian the Come Lady and we had laughed would have been a perfect time to come clean, to have told her about Sandra Faye. By the way, dear, while we're on the subject of laughs and sex, I lied about that historian lady. Or on the plane as we ate cold cuts and she had her hand on my leg. I could have confessed then. There were several other times I could have. Many, many several times.

But I had not. I finally decided, sitting there in my office that afternoon right after talking to Cow Baby Cowell, that I could not let the Sandra Faye lie live any longer. I would confess immediately. Yes, indeed. I would tell Jackie the whole story that very evening over dinner. We were already set to have a quiet dinner for two at the Somewhere over the Rainbow Café.

The Somewhere over the Rainbow Café on North May was a high-class hamburger place with white linen tablecloths and heavy silverware that was a shrine to Judy Garland, that magnificent singer. The owner was a former theater manager named Slezak who once had worked as a second-string promotion man on a Judy Garland singing tour of the country.

He'd come away from those three months in love forever and obsessed with her. He had recordings of her magnificent voice singing more than 120 songs, which he ran in sequence time after time all of the time in his restaurant. The food was good, but I loved going for the music almost as much. Has anybody ever sung a song better than Judy Garland sang "The Man That Got Away"? To name just one of the 120. The café walls were covered with movie posters and photographs of her at all ages, alone and with Fred Astaire, Gene Kelly, Mickey Rooney, James Mason, John Hodiak, John Payne, Dennis O'Keefe and the many other men she had starred with. The menu included seventeen kinds of hamburgers, ranging from the awful A Star Is Born Burger, which was raw hamburger meat between two pieces of French bread, to the wonderful You Made Me Love You Burger, three well-done patties layered with five pieces of sesame bun, four kinds of sliced cheese, lettuce, tomato, onion, olives, sweet and dill pickles, mustard, and three kinds of salad dressing—French, blue cheese and mayonnaise. Other burgers were covered with chili, with cottage cheese, with pizza sauce, with tunafish, with green and red peppers, with sour cream and chives. Some even had sweet things on them. The Easter Parade, for instance, was a burger with hot fudge sauce between two pieces of untoasted white bread. All were named for Judy Garland movies or songs.

By the time I parked the car and went in, I knew what I wanted. A Meet Me in St. Louis, which was an inch-thick burger between two pieces of sourdough bread, covered with bacon, tomato, cheddar cheese, black olives, dill pickles and Thousand Island dressing. I once had asked Slezak if there was any connection between the ingredients and St. Louis, and he'd said no.

Jackie was already there. I went over to the table, the one

we often had in the far northwest corner. I sat down, we kissed, and suddenly a young waiter in a tuxedo was there to tell us his name was George and to take our orders. I almost changed my mind and switched to a Wizard of Oz, which was the works—three patties, six pieces of sesame bun and a little bit of every topping they had, from mustard to chocolate, cottage cheese to blue cheese, chili to pizza sauce. Jackie shamed me by having just a Ring, Ring, Went the Bell, a burger topped only with melted Monterey Jack cheese and salsa on a sesame bun. So I stuck with a Meet Me in St. Louis.

Both of us had Diet Pepsis to drink. Jackie was not a drinker of alcohol, either.

Jackie was also very smart. And sometimes I am very easy to see through. So even before I had really settled into the first good bites of my sandwich she was onto the fact that I had something on my mind.

"What's up?" she kept asking. Over and over. Each time I would say nothing was up. Nothing. I suggested, in fact, that my problem was probably one of coming down. Down, down from my experience on the Short List. All I was really doing was waiting for the right moment, and we went on talking about matters other than my Sandra Faye Parsons lie. An editorial in *The Daily Oklahoman* that morning had come close to suggesting that the Democratic ticket of Griffin and Adair might very well turn the United States of America over to Evil Forces and Ideas that were not named. *The Daily Oklahoman* said that about all Democratic tickets.

And then, over coffee, when I was about to say, Jackie dear, there is something I have been meaning to tell you, she got me off track by making me mad.

"Hammerschmidt of Trailways called me today," she said.

"He said he was having some second thoughts and wondered if I still might be interested in the deal. I said no. He said fine and then said he had a favor to ask me to ask of you."

I said nothing about why in the world I would want to do a favor for Hammerschmidt.

"He wondered if you would mind making a speech at a bus convention in Portland, Oregon, in January. It would be to something like the National Association of Motor Bus Operators. They would pay you a fee, plus first-class airfare and a suite for two nights at the Portland Hilton. He wanted to know if you worked through a lecture bureau. I told him no, not yet."

"I thought my unsavory past had made me unsatisfactory to Mr. Hammerschmidt," I said.

"I said something about that to him and he said it had turned out differently than he had thought. People are coming into bus stations all over America asking if Lillian is going to be on board today. He mentioned the fact that he had met you to somebody in the bus association, and they asked him to see if you would speak. I guess they want to know if you have any other ideas for increasing the interest in intercity bus travel."

BUS SEX REVIVES INTERCITY BUS INDUSTRY!

I told her to tell him no speech, thank you.

And as the young waiter named George went off to run my Mastercharge card through a machine, I decided I would wait about ten years before telling Jackie about the Sandra Faye Parsons lie. Sometime in early 1986, maybe. Around late February or March, possibly.

By then I would surely have come up with a terrific explanation for why I had lied, something I really did not have right then. And in ten years it wouldn't really matter anymore, anyhow. I could even see the two of us having one huge laugh about it.

Jackie and I were proud of Tommy Walt's success as the founder and sole owner of our region's largest and finest restaurant grease collection service. His place of business had changed twice since he had begun five years before, with just him, a pickup truck, ten tin drums and one part-time employee. Now he had 127 employees and a fleet of forty-four trucks scattered around Oklahoma, North Texas, Arkansas, southern Kansas, and New Mexico. He had started in a dirty little run-down building that had once been used to store spices. Now he ran his company from a modern white-brick warehouse-garage-office near the stockyards in west Oklahoma City. He had built it from scratch with plans made by a real architect, and the end result, said Tommy Walt, was a facility that was state-of-the-art in the grease collection industry.

It was there I went late the next afternoon in my Buick Skylark.

I hit him at a bad time. He was in the middle of a crisis in North Texas. One of his trucks, loaded with seventeen twenty-gallon drums of old grease from fried chicken and hamburger restaurants and other eating establishments from Wichita Falls on the west to Greenville on the east, had been in a collision outside Sherman with a Frito-Lay semi on its way north from Dallas to Tulsa. The semi's trailer was full of potato chips, corn chips, Cheetos, various dips, sauces and other snack foods.

"It's a nightmare down there, Mack," said Tommy Walt. "Our grease is running all over the highway through torn bags of chips and ripped cans of bean dip and onion dip.

People and vehicles are tied up and sliding around. What are the odds of a truck of restaurant grease crashing into a Frito truck? They say it might take days to clean it up."

"Was anybody hurt?" I asked.

"No, Mack. Thank God."

Mack. He called me Mack. A couple of years ago he'd asked if he could. Calling one's father by his first name was not a typical Oklahoma thing to do. But he said it was crazy for him to call me Dad while everybody else in the state, young and old, smart and dumb, humble and prominent, called me Mack. What could I say? It was fine most of the time, but it did embarrass me when he did it around ordinary citizens. There was something not right about a son calling his father, a lieutenant governor of a state, by his first name in front of people.

I sat there on a couch in his office while he handled his crisis. He talked to emergency crews and backup crews, to the Texas highway patrol, to insurance adjusters and newspaper reporters. I read for the tenth time or so the framed citations on the wall behind his desk that designated him the 1973 Oklahoma Jaycee of the Year, the 1974 Oklahoma Entrepreneur of the Year, the 1975 president of NAGC, the National Association of Grease Collectors, and similar honored things.

He kept apologizing for keeping me waiting, and I could not help but think how quickly things had changed in my life. From having lunch as a veep Short-Lister in a room of wine bottles with Richardson McKinney, to this. All in a few days. God Bless America.

Finally things quieted down and he said to me: "Dad, I have an idea, a business idea, a proposition."

Dad?

"Remember that when I started you didn't like the name T.W. Grease Collectors?" he said. I remembered. Both Jackie and I had felt something a little more dignified might have been better. I'd suggested Golden Plate Collections. "Well, I have been thinking about doing with my business what Mom and McDonald's and Wendy's and 7-Eleven and many others have done with theirs. I am talking franchising. There is no reason in the world why the same good business principles I have followed in setting up and running this business should not be nationwide. But running it all from here as one big company is not the practical way. Why not franchises?"

I was not sure if that was a question, but I said, "Sounds good to me, son."

"The problem has always been how to do it, what to use as a handle," he continued. "And that, Dad, is where you come in. That is what you can now provide."

Dad?

"What if I changed the name of my company to One-Eyed Mack Collections? You are a national figure now. It would immediately gain attention with the public and thus with potential franchisees. It seems like a natural to me. What do you think?"

I did not think anything. I could not think anything. I could not think at all.

Tommy Walt said: "I am talking a straight business deal. So much in a flat fee or so much a percentage of the franchise business for the use of your name."

I remained silent.

"Look, I know this is a shocker," said Tommy Walt. "Talk to Mom about it or whatever, but believe me, I think this is something that will work. Look what fried chicken did for a colonel named Sanders. There's not a person in America who would not recognize the name or face of the Colonel. Not a person. It could be the same for you, Dad, for a lieutenant governor named Mack. I foresee the time when there would be a One-Eyed Mack Collections operation in every city and town of any size in America. We could get a really great artist to do a kind of special drawing of you that would be the company trademark, like Mom has of her for JackieMarts."

I stood up.

"Well?" said Tommy Walt from the other side of the desk. "What do you think?"

I said: "Son, I admire your entrepreneurial mind and spirit. I really do. But I am the lieutenant governor of Oklahoma, a public official, a servant of the people. Being on the Short List for two days does not change that. I cannot rent out my name and my picture for commercial purposes."

"Even to your son?"

"Even to my son."

"Well, you can't blame a guy for trying, can you?"

I agreed with him, waved good-bye and headed for his office door, as he took another call about the collision outside Sherman, Texas, between a truck full of restaurant grease and a truck full of Fritos and other snack foods.

"Thanks for coming by, Mack," he hollered after me.

12

. . .

BLAH-BLAH-BOOM

The next morning Arneson and Heket turned up at my office. They were Oklahoma's most powerful Democratic leaders and had just returned from New York City and the convention. It seemed strange in retrospect that I had not laid eyes on either of them or any other member of the Oklahoma delegation in New York except from the podium. But what had happened to me had happened so fast and so peculiarly that there simply had been no opportunity for such normal things as being with my political friends from home.

Arneson and Heket had been important players in an important happening earlier in my life. As young dynamo movers in the Democratic Party of Oklahoma—the press then called them Party Stalwarts—they had flown into Adabel on a private plane one afternoon and interviewed me. It had been part of a search for Democratic candidates for statewide office. I had attracted some attention as a one-eyed county commissioner because of the way I had gotten some war statues built on our county courthouse lawn. Arneson and Heket had asked me what statewide office I might be interested in. "Lieutenant governor," I had replied, to their surprise. "Nobody ever wants to be lieutenant governor," one of them said. It was a while later, after two earlier choices for lieutenant governor to run with Joe Hayman of Buffalo had fallen by the wayside because of corruption or personal-habit problems, that they had come back to me with a concrete proposal.

Now here they were again. Arneson was still a lawyer from Woodward out in northwestern Oklahoma, but he was also the chairman of the Oklahoma Democratic Party. He seemed pretty much the same, except that most of his hair was gone and his suit was more expensive-looking. Heket was a Tulsa oilman who had appeared rich the first time I met him, and he still did. The main changes in him were that his black hair had turned road-gravel gray and his stomach was now the size and shape of a small watermelon. He was the Democratic national committeeman from Oklahoma.

I had them sit down, and we did some rehashing of my great moments in the national sun and talked about the mummy search and other things before they got down to business. By the time they did, I had already figured out what was coming.

Heket said:

"We believe it's time to move the party on to another era in state politics. Let's call it the Mack Era."

"You have in the last few days become the star of Oklahoma," said Arneson. "Politics is a business of stars. You are it."

"It?" I asked.

"It for governor," said Heket.

I barely had enough time to say how honored and humbled I was at their incredibly surprising choice of me to lead Oklahoma and the Democratic Party into a new era, when Arneson brought up what he called "a need to clarify before proceeding."

He said:

"Let me get right to it, Mack. Heket and I remember that conversation we had with you down in Adabel years ago. We both remember how pleased we were that you said right out that you wanted to be lieutenant governor. We both remember, because we talked to a lot of people around the state on that particular trip, and you were the only one interested in being lieutenant governor. There were several who said they'd like to be president and senator and governor and even a handful who wanted to be state auditor or treasurer and the like. But you, only you, Mack, said lieutenant governor. Heket and I remember remarking to each other back on the plane that there were not many people around whose ambition it was to be lieutenant governor of Oklahoma."

Heket picked it up from there and dropped it on me.

"So this business about the convict in Missouri is troubling. We heard what you said at the press conference in New York, and as far as we are concerned that closes the book. But we have to know before we get into any kind of campaign situation if there is any more to it than that. We have to know, Mack, if there are any little corners, any tiny loops or leaps in the story that are still waiting out there to come out. We simply have to know, for reasons that I think are obvious."

I said:

"There is no more to it than what I said. When you two asked me about what office, I said lieutenant governor almost automatically. It was because of Pepper. It was in my mind because of Pepper and Big Bo. But it was because of Pepper, not because of any desire to eventually pardon Big Bo." I held up my right hand as if taking an oath. "So help me God."

"May I ask," Arneson said, "why in the hell you did not tell us about that convict thing then?"

"Because it did not have anything to do with what was going on. Like I said, so help me God."

"Well, that pretty well does it, then," Arneson said. He turned to Heket. "Agreed?"

"Can you take the heat on it in a campaign?" Heket asked.

"Yes, sir," I said. "But what about all of that other stuff? Aren't you worried about that, too?"

"No, sir. None of it's a problem for the people of Oklahoma," Arneson said. "All of that bothers only reporters and the Nationals."

Arneson stood. Heket joined him. So did I.

"Congratulations," Arneson said. "We look forward to the Mack Era of Democratic politics in Oklahoma.

"What about Joe?" I asked.

"He steps aside, or you run against him," said Heket.

"Have you talked to him?"

"We thought we'd leave that to you," Arneson said.

"Thanks," I said.

C., as usual, came with a story from the recent annals of Oklahoma crime.

"A kid walked into the Coca-Cola plant in Ponca City the other night. He was carrying one of those little toy pistols that look like forty-fives and wearing a plastic Robert Redford mask. It's amazing what they can do with plastic these days, Mack. Both the gun and the mask looked very realistic, although the people at the plant knew it wasn't really Robert

Redford. They were right in the middle of a bottling run on Tab.

"The kid comes over to them and says it's a stickup. He demands all their money and their watches. The guys on the bottling line think maybe it's a joke, because holding up bottling plants is not a common thing, even in Ponca City. One of them grabs a handful of Tab bottle caps and throws them at the kid. The kid panics, forgets his gun isn't real, threatens to kill everyone, pulls the trigger, and nothing happens. The Tab guys—there are about six of them—notice, of course. They rush the kid, take away his gun and tie him up. Then they take him in the back where the Tab comes out of some kind of vat into pipes and on down the line to where the empty bottles are. They tap into it with some kind of little hose and put the open end down the throat of the kid. Funny joke, show him a lesson, and all of that. But the thing gets out of hand, and before you know it the kid has choked to death.

"Now the six Tab guys panic. Instead of calling the cops, they decide to try to get away with it. They take the body out back and put it under an old paint tarp in the bed of one guy's Dodge pickup and go back inside to finish their shift. The idea is that later they will bury the body or weight it down with rocks and things and throw it in the river. When they come back, the truck is missing. Somebody has stolen it. It turns up abandoned an hour later near Perry. A sheriff's deputy finds it, finds the body, traces the truck to one of the Tab guys. He squeals like new tires on his five buddies, and justice triumphs over evil once again."

"I can't imagine a worse way to die than choking on Tab," I said. "It tastes like carbonated cough syrup."

"That's not all of the story," C. said. "It turns out the kid was the son of a Coca-Cola route man who was laid up at home with a bad back. One of those disk things. He had told his son those guys on the bottling line cheated him out of two hundred fifty-five dollars he had won in a Monday Night Football pool there at the plant."

We were in the backseat of C.'s Lincoln, eating lunch. He had insisted on trying a Chinese fast-food place, so we had gone to Oklahoma Nanking Express #4 on Broadway. He had something awful, a mixture of hard-boiled egg and half-cooked fish that smelled to high heaven. I got two egg rolls and a carton of sweet-and-sour pork. The carton was made of weak white cardboard, so my hands were quickly a mess of sweet-and-sour sauce.

"I really do hate this stuff," I said to C.

"It'll grow on you," he said.

"No it won't, because I am never having any of it again."

He smiled, took another plastic-fork bite of his awful lunch and said, "What about Mexican, then, next time?"

"Anything but this."

The main business of the lunch was my future. Do I or do I not run for governor? And what about Joe, whom I had an appointment to see right after our lunch?

Jackie's advice was, Run. Everyone I had talked to about it, in fact, had said, Run. They all used the basic Arneson–Heket line. That I had become a superstar of Oklahoma, and stars do not burn as brightly as mine had for too long, so the time was now. Joe would probably step aside gladly, citing health reasons, and it was time for him to move on to other things, anyhow.

C. preached more of the same, only a bit more directly.

"Look, Mack, it boils down to this: The Chip is an idiot. He always has been and he always will be. He's slick and he's smart and he knows how to get elected, but that isn't all there should be to it. Name one thing constructive or different he has done for the state. You can't. All he does is just be governor. That's it. You are not an idiot, Mack. You would do more than just be governor."

"C., my friend, you are dreaming if you believe I have some kind of heavy-duty master plan to transform Oklahoma into something else, like California or paradise," I said. "I'm good at just being lieutenant governor, like Joe is at just being governor. I have nothing else in mind."

"You'll come up with something. You're also a good human being. The Governor's Office could use one of those for a while, even if you don't do one damned thing."

C. was my friend.

My own thinking was a mess. Sure, I would love to be governor of Oklahoma. Who in his right mind wouldn't? But I had always prided myself on not being one of those people who kidded themselves into thinking they were something they were not. Joe had been right when he'd said I was an accident. I really was just a guy from Kansas with a junior college education who'd come to Oklahoma by accident and lucked into being county commissioner and now lieutenant governor. It always seemed to me that that was about as high as God's plan for me called for. Before New York, I never, ever went to sleep at night dreaming about being governor. I promise. Joe used to say that there wasn't a politician of either party, of either sex, of either honest or crooked bent who didn't think of running for the next-higher office the split second he won his first election. "Show me a justice of the peace fresh from victory at the polls," he said, "and I'll show you a man who's thinking about the type of toilet seats he wants in his White House." Not me.

Joe was an extremely serious problem for me. I am not

going to comment on C.'s opinion of him. Or Jackie's opinion of him. Or even *The Daily Oklahoman*'s or the *Tulsa World*'s. I have never made a public comment of a negative type about Joe Hayman, and I am not about to start now. He was what he was and part of what he was was the man who had made it possible for me to be the Second Man of Oklahoma and, let's face it, to have my incredible moments in the national sun with David Brinkley, the mummy and all the rest.

All of this was running through my mind as C.'s driver, OBI special agent Randy Pogue, wheeled the Lincoln into the circle driveway in front of the Governor's Mansion.

The Governor's Mansion. It was a real three-story mansion built in the late 1920s, of the same kind of gray limestone as the capitol building. It had a terrific red-tile roof, and inside there were plenty of bedrooms and sitting rooms and even a ballroom on the third floor. There were also lots of nice furniture, knickknacks and chandeliers.

Jackie would love living here, I said to myself as I got out of the car under the white-columned portico. So would the kids. So would I.

Who in his right mind wouldn't?

Joe received me in the second-floor sitting room, just off the master bedroom. He was in sport clothes, an open shirt and slacks. I heard the sound of a woman singing "God Bless America" coming faintly from somewhere. Was it a record of Kate Smith, a tape of Jill? Was Jill off down the hall singing it live as some kind of attempt to spook me?

"Sorry you had to come over here, Mack," Joe said. "But the doctors want me to wait another week or so before I hit the office and the rest like old times. It'll be another week or so."

"Always great to come over here to the mansion," I said.

"Don't get too fond of it," he said, "if you know what I mean. I was at the window just now. I saw you giving the place the eye. Giving the eye for what kind of new toilet seats you might want. I saw you."

I decided only to grin in response.

There were several newspapers on a coffee table in front of his chair, and apparently he had been reading them. And rereading them. I noticed that the ones on top were *The Daily Oklahoman* and *Tulsa World*.

"Sounds like it was some parade Johnny Potts threw for you. Sorry I couldn't make it. I caught that press conference of yours in New York. Good job, Mack. Good job."

I thanked him and sat down in the chair across from his. It was a hard-backed chair he had set out for me to use. It made me think of Bill Murray, one of our governors from the past, who had had the chair in front of his desk in the governor's office nailed to the floor. That was so politicians and others who wished to move their chair closer in an act of chumminess could not do so. Murray loved to watch their looks of frustration as they tried in vain to do so.

"What was it like, Mack?" Joe said after a few moments. "What was it like being so close? Did you ever let yourself go all the way? Did you think about being called Mr. Vice-President? Did you see your name in all the almanacs and history books now and forevermore? Did you think about what it would be like to be the Second Man of America, to be a heartbeat away from being president, from being the most powerful man in the world? The most powerful man in the world, Mack? Did you allow yourself to have these thoughts? Tell me about them."

At first I thought he was putting me on. Making fun of me. Reminding me of what I had lost and what I had that should have been his. It was all very confusing. I finally decided to take him seriously.

"No, Joe, I never had a chance really to have all of that," I replied, honestly. "It came and went so fast, and I had so many fires to put out, I just never had the time to think, Wow, me Second Man of America maybe. The whole thing lasted barely two days, remember."

"Oh, I remember, Mack. I really do remember. I will always remember that, Mack. Always."

I knew then that we had arrived at the time to talk about what I was there to talk about and what he knew I was there to talk about.

I opened my mouth to say something like, "I assume you've read the stories about me running for governor...."

But before I could get anything out, he said, "I've read the stories about people far and wide wanting you to run for governor. Are you going to? Did you come here now to tell me? If that's it, tell me. Go ahead, Mack. Say, 'Joe, our days as a Super Sooner team for Oklahoma are over.' Go ahead, Mack. Go ahead."

"I have not decided anything of the kind, Joe. There is nothing I would like to do less than run against you. You must know that. You have been like a big brother to me. You and Arneson and Heket took me out of that county commissioner's job in Adabel and put me on your ticket...."

"So your answer is yes. Is that it? Is it yes from Arneson and Heket, too?"

"Not exactly. I would feel awful running against you, Joe. I really would. Maybe there is some alternative to that. I know Arneson and Heket feel the same way."

"Like maybe my stepping aside for you? Like my calling a little news conference to announce that for health and other reasons I have decided not to seek reelection, and in my stead I am delighted and proud to endorse the candidacy of my friend the lieutenant governor, the famous friend of misplaced mummies, The One-Eyed Mack? Is that an acceptable alternative?"

"It sure is, obviously. That would be great."

Joe got up from his comfortable chair and stood off to the side like he was a furniture salesman. "Let's say this is the chair of the governor of Oklahoma. This chair is the chair you want, right, Mack? My chair. The governor's chair. Well, let me tell you, sir, that if you want it, you will have to take it. I am not giving it up to you or anyone else without a fight. No, sirree. Not without a fight. I have earned this chair, and I will keep this chair until I decide to give it up or the people take it away from me."

He dropped his voice to a whisper and held onto that chair with his left hand so hard the knuckle turned the color of dirty snow.

"You, my dear one-eyed friend, and Arneson and Heket and the big-city creeps at *The Daily Oklahoman* and the *World* and the whatsoevers everywhere else in this state are not going to be able to snap your fingers and say, 'Get your butt out of there, Buffalo Joe. Get your butt out of there, Buffalo Joe.' I didn't get it in in the first place letting people do that to me, and I am not giving it up that way."

"I hear you, Buffalo Joe."

" 'I hear you, Buffalo Joe.' What does that mean? For God's sake, what does that mean?"

"It means . . . I don't know what it means."

He moved behind the chair and leaned down across the back toward me.

"Let me see if I can help you come to grips with what it

means. Let me say to you now in words that both of us will understand: I am not stepping aside. I am not going quietly. If you decide to oppose me for the Democratic nomination for governor of this state, I will oppose you with every ounce of energy, every dollar and dime, every tactic and strategy I can muster. I will hold back nothing, I will shrink from nothing. Politics is getting elected. Nobody cares what you do, as long as you win. There are no no-nos, Mack. No rules."

"What are you saying, for God's sake?"

"I am saying, for God's sake, that what has come out about you since this Short List thing came up will look like Church of the Holy Road Sunday-school stuff by the time I get through. Questions, Mack. I'll have lots of questions. Oh, Mack, will I ever have questions.

"Why does a man change his name? If he'll change his name, what else about himself will he change?

"Valium from Cal Blackwell. I hear from Johnny Potts that they got some ex–city cop who says he sold it to Cal. Do we want a governor who uses illicit drugs and who associates with people who associate with drug dealers? Cal Blackwell offered me a Valium when we were in New York. I said no. My opponent, the lieutenant governor, said yes. What does that say about the difference between us? What does it say?

"That stolen speech. You were in charge of that speech. I asked you to supervise Cow Cowell. Doesn't Cow Cowell have a reputation for smoking pot? Hey, what are all of these drug associations of the lieutenant governor's all about, anyhow?

"What about that movie they made up in Enid? It's nothing but dirt and filth. It's pornography. Now, I asked the lieutenant governor to stop it. But it didn't stop. Don't let the change of the name to *Arkansas Parts* fool you, voters of Oklahoma. Now, do we want as governor a man who supports the making of screw movies in our clean and wholesome State of Oklahoma?

"Another thing, voters of Oklahoma. Do you want a governor who on state time went over and cavorted in France somewhere? France! Cavorting in France!"

I said: "I was there trying to get the speaker of the Oklahoma House of Representatives to come home, and you know it. What do you mean by 'cavort', anyhow?"

"We'll let the voters of Oklahoma decide what 'cavort' means. That is what we will do. Confusion about that eye injury? Why would stories about being a war hero or being some kind of big-league baseball player turn up? Who plants such figments in somebody's biography? Who was it who posed for that picture down at Iwo, anyhow? Who was it who told that reporter some cock-and-bull story about Stan Musial? Does my opponent have a problem with exaggeration? Does he have a problem with the truth?

"And what about that bus thing? Have there been other women on other buses? What does it say about a man that he buys sex from a stranger on a motor vehicle, a public conveyance for taking little children to their grandmothers— and vice versa? If a man would do that, what would he not do? Do we want our state to be run by a man who would do that kind of thing?

"I might even call for you to come forward and confess your other sins. All of these came out in just under two days. What might another two days of looking around turn up? There wasn't a lot of time between the time your wife's first husband died in Korea and the time the two of you married. . . . "

"Joe, you are despicable!" I was on my feet.

"Go ahead. Come over here and hit me. It will make a great story. How the lieutenant governor, his ego raised and crazed by being on the vice-presidential Short List for two days, turns like an attack dog on his old friend and political benefactor the still recovering Governor Joe Hayman. Oh, I mustn't forget the old convict in Missouri. Everybody who believes that story of yours will fit into one phone booth, by the time I get through asking my questions about that..."

"This is blackmail, Joe. You are blackmailing me."

"Yes, sir. That's what it's called, Mack. I like being governor of Oklahoma. I want to stay being governor of Oklahoma. You are my friend. It is nothing personal."

"Nothing personal? You would bring Jackie into this. You would publicly accuse me of everything from being a wicked name-changer to a sex fiend and an adulterer, and you say it's not personal?"

"It's politics. Politics is the only place where clean people can be dirty in public and stay clean. There's nothing the voters would love more than a real dirty one between Buffalo Joe and The One-Eyed Mack. The press would go crazy for it. I mean crazy. You know I'm right."

I was already at the door. "You are one despicable human being, Joe. I mean despicable. I mean bottom-of-the-barrel rottenness. You make the air you breathe smell putrid. You are putrid."

"If you don't run and you stay lieutenant governor, I'll appoint you chairman of a governor's commission to find the missing mummy. We'll have to come up with something catchy to go with it. A slogan or something. Mummy Sooner? Or Mummy Oklahoma. Something like that, right. Mummy Oklahoma, Mack. Mummy Oklahoma."

Suddenly his face looked exactly like Cow Cowell's, with the need for something right between the eyes. I had never in my life been so angry. Never.

He wasn't through. "My mother sent me a pair of slippers as a get-well gift," he said. "They're brown vinyl, rabbit fur inside. The size is small. Mine is large. My big toe barely fits into them. To show there's no hard feelings, they're yours, Mack, if you want them."

I slammed the door so hard behind me that I was sure windows would crack, vases would crash, paintings and mirrors would fall. But I did not hear anything.

Not even the sound of "God Bless America."

The Governor's Mansion was on 23rd Street, in the next block east from the capitol. Special Agent Pogue and C. had gone on in the Lincoln, of course, so I walked back across Santa Fe Road and onto the east parking lot toward the capitol. My mind was on Joe and me and what had just happened.

"Lewt Guv," somebody said. I looked up. Yes, it was him. Jed Berryhill of the dirty movies.

"Can I talk to you a minute?" he said, walking up to me.

"No," I said, not stopping or even making eye contact.

He fell in beside me and strode along with me anyhow.

"I know we had some differences," he said. "But we must let bygones be bygones so we can create something beautiful together."

We arrived at the side door of the building. I just kept walking. So did he. And talking.

"Your story is the story of the year. What a picture it will make! All I want now is an option. Let me go back to Hollywood, where it all happens, and let me make it happen.

It is a dynamite natural. Handicapped lieutenant governor goes to national political convention. Lightning strikes. Makes speech. Becomes national hero. We may have to do something about the ending, but I'm telling you, it's all there. It's *Mr. Smith Goes to Washington* all over again. *Mr. Mack Goes to New York*. It's got it all."

I still had not turned my right eye in his direction. We were on the marble steps, headed to the second floor and my office.

"I'll get Bob to play you," Berryhill said.

There was no way I could resist saying, "Bob?"

"Redford. Bob Redford. I almost did an environmental short with him."

Now, at my office door, I stopped.

"I know where you can get a mask of him to use instead."

"What? What do you mean?"

"You are not going in here," I said. "You are not going anywhere with me, now or any other time."

"That's a no on the option, then? What about the mummy story? Who owns the right to it? It's a natural. We'll get Jerry to play the mummy."

I left him there at the door, not even caring to know who Jerry was.

The walk from the Governor's Mansion to my office took only five minutes. Even with Berryhill rattling in my ear, I had been able to think about what was really important. I was still able to make a decision. In fact, there was really no decision to make.

I did not want to be governor of Oklahoma that badly. I couldn't imagine anyone in the world who would.

In fact, the more I thought about it, the more I realized

again what a truly wonderful challenge, honor and opportunity it was to be the lieutenant governor of Oklahoma, and how truly wonderful I was at doing it.

Making the Short List had not changed any of that.

Behind the closed door of my office, I removed my suitcoat and took off the concealed "wire"—a tiny microphone and cassette recorder—that C. had had Special Agent Pogue, his top electronics man, strap on me. He had insisted I wear it on the chance Joe tried to pull a fast one. "Who knows," C. said, "he might even be stupid enough to try to blackmail you. If he does, we will have him dead zero in the water."

Now I opened the recorder and removed the tiny little cassette, which wasn't much larger than a pack of matches. I took a ballpoint pen from my desk and stripped all of the tape out of the cassette. Then with a pair of scissors, I cut the tape into many shreds and tossed them into my wastebasket.

I really did not want to be governor of Oklahoma that badly.

And I really could not imagine anyone in his right mind who would.

Blah-blah-boom.